D1488874

The Forest Speaks: Book 1 Awakening the Rose

By

Diomira Rose D'Agostino

Copyright © 2014 by Diomira Rose D'Agostino

All rights reserved.

Book design by Diomira Rose D'Agostino

No part of this book may be reproduced in any form or by any
electronic or mechanical means including information storage and
retrieval systems, without permission in writing from the author.
The only exception is by a reviewer, who may quote short excerpts
in a review.

Faery Light, LLC books are available for order through Ingram
Press Catalogues

This book is a work of fiction. Names, characters, places, and
incidents either are products of the author's imagination or are
used fictitiously. Any resemblance to actual persons, living or
dead, events, or locales is entirely coincidental.

Diomira Rose D'Agostino
Visit my website at www.diomirarose.com

Printed in the United States of America
First Printing: August 2014
Published by Sojourn Publishing, LLC

ISBN: 978-1-62747-069-8
Ebook ISBN: 978-1-62747-070-4
LCN: Pending

–The Forest Speaks–

"A gentle story that tiptoes into the wonder-filled reality of nature and the trees. It helps remind us that we, as humans, are not alone, but a vital part of the miraculous wonder of all Life. The Word has always been: 'Be still and know that I am God.' Nature, and especially the trees that the native tribes call 'Standing People,' have always known and honored this. Would that all of us could remember also!"

–Rev. Marian Young Starnes
Founder of Terra Nova Center and
Brigade of Light, Author of
Letters from Summerland

Dedication

To the Faeries who throughout time have demonstrated their commitment to support the Earth as she grows in consciousness by shining their Faery Light even at night while most are asleep. They seek to help us remember so we can take our rightful place as fully realized co-creator divine beings in the great Plan of Creation.

To those brave human souls who have sought to maintain a conscious connection to the Earth and all her creatures.

May we continue to work together as we all remember who we are and awaken to our own truth and inner spark of Divinity!

Acknowledgments

T here are so many to thank who have either directly or indirectly made this book a possibility. I want to thank some of my dear friends and soul sisters who have walked with me through many obstacles throughout many lifetimes: Noelle Abent, you are the most kind and caring person that I know. Thank you for your friendship, your support and your completely nonjudgmental acceptance and love. Betty Estremera, we have shared so many lifetimes together. Thank you for walking with me side by side once again as we explore the Earth, the Stars and Beyond. Lisa Peacock, I love you! Thank you for wonderfully stimulating and uplifting spiritual dialogue by faery light! I know I can always be just me with you. Kristin Quarles, thank you for reminding me to play, whether walking through the woods or going down the Rabbit Hole, it is always another adventure in the Land of Spirit. Christa Lamos, thank you for your ability to love me deeply and see me. Let's not forget your humor that is magical beyond measure!

Thank you to Johnny Balestreire who supported me tirelessly through the whole writing process. You always encouraged me to continue regardless of the outer circumstances that presented themselves. You were my friend and partner, and you acted as a rock that kept me grounded when I quite possibly could have flown away.

I also want to thank Inner Quest Church for all the love and support they give freely, for this organization is truly a center of God's love in these transformational times. It has been a beacon in my darkest hours and a support system and cheerleader in times of great joy. In particular, I want to acknowledge Cindy Fuller who has been my teacher, my mentor, my spiritual advisor, but also my friend. She has been a huge force that has helped me learn to navigate matter and understand this earthly experience from an energetic perspective. Above all, I truly honor the connection we both share with the faerie realm. I remember!

I want to honor Terra Nova Spiritual Center – a place where I feel at home. Thank you to Rev. Marian Young Starnes who I call Mother Marian because of her open arms always welcoming me home.

I also want to honor and thank my mother, Diane. It was your open-mindedness that allowed me to be free to explore many paths growing up. It was you who instilled in me the belief and knowing of the Faeries.

Thank you to Tom Bird, Gwen Payne and Rama for helping me cross the finish line!

I would like to express gratitude to Infinite Spirit for everything that comes through me. I realize more and more each day that I am just a vessel through which the Divine can express. I also wish to thank my spiritual team of angels, guides and teachers. Bless you for your patience, unconditional love and commitment to assisting me as I move through this physical experience here on the beautiful planet Earth.

And most of all, and with a heart full of love and joy, I thank all of the beautiful faery beings! I am so blessed by the profound connection that we share. I hope that our relationship continues to grow and deepen each and every single day. Thank you for sharing your love, light, wisdom, and creativity with me. Thank you for being my friends and companions, and when needed, my boss.

Table of Contents

Introduction

This story came to me on a gentle breeze. It rose up from deep within my heart and soul, and was sung to me over and over again until I heard it very clearly. Years ago I believed my first book would be a nonfiction autobiographical account of my journey. What came to me instead was the book that is before you. And although it has many real life components (it is up to you to decide which ones those are), it is, after all, fiction!

I wrote this book over a period of a year! I say book, and not story, because as you will see when you come to the end, that this is only the beginning of the story! I am already well into the second book, and I expect that there will at least be three.

I began the writing of this book on March 23, 2013. I was at Dancing Bear Lodge, a friend's cabin, in Blairsville, Georgia. I had decided to seclude myself for a weekend to begin the writing process. I knew there was no better way to get started. I would like to share with you an entry out of my journal from that day:

March 23, 2013

Here I am at Dancing Bear Lodge. I am overjoyed to be here again. Having just completed a beautiful sacred ceremony in which I set my intention for this weekend, all of my spiritual cohorts have been welcomed to join me in celebration. We danced my altar into being. The altar I set up contains aspects of the four elements to represent the universal balance of all Life, and to honor the Creator in all Its myriad forms. Divine Mother/Father God, I love You! I come to You as Your daughter, surrendered and vowing to serve Thee. My heart opens and pours out offerings at Your feet. I am so blessed.

I look up and realize how many miracles abound in my life. I am so grateful to have this beautiful haven of warmth and nurturing shared with me. As I sit back and contemplate it all, I am made aware of how auspicious this really is! This is no accident that I am here. This is the fourth time I've been here: four for balance, new foundation, the four directions, four corners, four elements.

Even more significant than that, though, there is something else that comes to mind. This is where I first received the message that I was to work with the Nature Realm. This is where the Voice of Nature truly spoke to me for the first time. It was back in 2008 at a meditation retreat. At the beginning of that event we all drew cards to receive a message for that weekend. Mine said that I would remember something from childhood. What could it be?

I carried on and didn't give it thought beyond that. By the end of the retreat, I had completely forgotten about the message. On the last day, we were invited to do a powerful meditation in which we were instructed to go out in nature alone. We were to let go of the old and release all that no longer served us on our path. I sat down on the ground near a tree, and made myself comfortable. I began to follow the steps of this releasing process. I could feel layers and layers just melting off me into the Earth. I allowed the Mother Earth to pull off this excess weight I'd been carrying around with me. After some time (I don't really know how much time had passed – maybe 20 minutes, maybe more) I could feel an ebbing occur. I could tell the process was coming to completion.

Then I was empty. There was so much space. That's when I heard the voice speak to me, and yet at the same time it was like an instant knowing: "It's time to remember! Remember and begin to work with the Faerie and Crystal Kingdoms!" Oh my! How could I have forgotten? So there it was around my 26th birthday that I came to remember my divine purpose. And So It Was.

And so it is four and a half years later that I sit here, having fully embraced and embarked on this journey. And I never looked back. I am a healer, a teacher, and a channel. And today I sit ready to write! Ready to write their story, and ready to write my own. I love them!

That day, many moons ago, was an initiation. An initiation onto the path of awakening to my True Self and to remembering who I am. Today is another initiation. For today I leave one chapter, and step into another. I have now come full circle. Today I start the writing of the journey – although the journey will be written from many perspectives, not just my own. For my journey is only a small part of the story. As I move forward I come to understand that this journey is not just about me. It's about everyone. It's about all those who worked with me – those known and unknown. I open the space and invite those who have shared in this work to come forward now. Let us write our story. Let us open our hearts, awaken our souls and dance! Let us dance together as we weave an ancient tale for all to hear, touch, and feel. Let us tell the story: **The Forest Speaks**

This is a journey into the world of Nature. Nature exists on many levels – it is not just what you see "outside". Nature is comprised of all form and the energy behind it; it is the harmonious balance of things in motion. Nature is Life.

When we enter this world we must cross the bridge from our mind into our heart. From there the possibilities are endless. The cosmos is the limit.

Imagine a world where all life works together for the greater good – where life vibrates and flows in harmony. Humans, animals, plants, and faeries work together under the direction of Creator for the good of the whole.

Well, that world already exists. We have just forgotten it – we have just stepped outside of the Garden because we wanted to have an experience of our own.

It is now time, as we move in tandem with the Great Cycles of Time, to step back into alignment with all of creation – for we were never separate, but the veil we created has made us think and feel that we are.

It is time to remember who we are. It is time to remember why we came here and what we are meant to do and be. I do not pretend to have these answers for you. But these answers and more will all be revealed to you when you turn within to your heart.

Sometimes we need only a little nudge of inspiration for this remembrance to occur. This story can activate that seemingly forgotten memory from deep within. Perhaps like a small stepping stone in that direction, this story is akin to a gentle bridge that can help us enter the magical realm that lies within our hearts.

The Story of the Forest is a timeless tale that contains within it many stories, for everything has a story to tell. Each story has many gifts, treasures, and lessons.

We must only stop to listen.

Prologue

"One sees clearly only with the heart. Anything essential is invisible to the eyes."

—Antoine De Saint Exupery, *The Little Prince*

M oonlight struck the land, emitting a soft, vibrant glow. The Forest trees were breathing in harmony with the sun and the moon. The flowers shimmered like a thousand tiny jewels that dotted the moss-covered twisted tree roots. Shades of colors never before seen on the known spectrum of visible light sparkled throughout the Forest floor. Everything was teeming with the movement of life as it swirled to the beautiful melodic song coming from everywhere.

A shining figure could be discerned amongst the trees. The moving form gleamed in the moonlight that danced off the Great Oak. A group of younger oak trees formed a perfect circle around the Old One, as the Great Oak was often called. A raven, black as night, sat perched upon the highest branch of the Old One, unwilling to miss a single moment of the spectacle before him. The luminescent figure twirled from one tree to the next, then back again to the Old One in the center. Each pirouette was an act of expression in rhythm to a song only audible to "those with ears to hear" it. The figure wore upon her form a gossamer gown that flowed with her movements—or was it the light of the moon that danced around her? One couldn't be sure!

Within this perfectly formed ring of trees, the Divine Mother's energy emanated from all directions, engulfing anyone who entered. It was here in this circle that Mother Earth whispered her secrets. To know her in this way was to be held inside her heart and become one with her love, one with her heartbeat.

Elsewhere…

A tiny soft bluish light flickered in the night. The dew gave off a shimmering glow against the light of the moon. Somewhere in the distance, the gurgling of a babbling brook was audible as it made its way through the glen at the edge of the Forest. A frog was just beginning his twilight serenade, and a mushroom peaked out from under a leaf where light rain droplets made a pitter-pattering sound just overhead. The tiny light flickered again as it floated with intended purpose a few feet ahead.

Then there were two tiny twinkling lights. To and fro they danced as if to some unheard song. Perhaps they danced to the ballad the frog sang for the mushroom for the first time in several millennia. Perhaps they danced to something else.

The tiny lights could have been mistaken for fireflies if one did not take special care to notice. One possessing a sharp eye would not be fooled, however. For an astute one would clearly recognize the pastel colors of pink and powder blue that emanated from these tiny orbs, quickly distinguishing them from any known lightning bug. The Night Forest's song continued on, and the tiny lights continued floating in rhythm to this sweet otherworldly melody all too keen for most humans to hear; but "those with ears to hear" could perceive the intoxicating sound of strumming harp strings and wild wind chimes reverberating off lily pads and being carried by the mist. In perfect synch, a spellbinding liquid voice rose up as if from everywhere and nowhere all at the same time.

Then, just as suddenly as the music had commenced, all became reverently silent, as if in some gesture that said, "Awaken...!"

Chapter 1
Dreaming Awake

*"The future belongs to those who believe in the
power of their dreams."*

—Eleanor Roosevelt

Maine – 2004

T he bright rays of sunlight shone through the
curtain, completely uninvited on this Monday
morning. *The nerve of that golden disc in the sky...* she
thought in a half-playful manner as she brushed a strand
of golden brown hair out of her face. She peeled one
eyelid open, revealing eyes that rivaled the sky in their
blueness. Stealing a peek at her alarm clock, she read
the bright red digital numbers: 6:15.

A scowl arose across her face. She pulled the covers
over her head in disgust. She had a good twenty
minutes before she had to get up and get ready for
school. Another scowl came across her face at the
thought of that horribly boring and annoyingly
mandatory institution. Jedda wasn't sure what it was

that she didn't like about it. The teachers were nice enough. She really was quite fond of Miss Silverton, her history teacher. She supposed that Mr. Ramen was agreeable as well. And aside from making her feel like she was surrounded by giants, the kids weren't all that bad either. They weren't mean or anything—just tall, very tall. Jedda was smaller than average. Not just for her age but in comparison to the human race. She always had been, and seeing as she was now almost sixteen, it wasn't looking like that was ever going to change.

Regardless of how nice everyone was, Jedda kept to herself more often than not. It wasn't that she didn't like anyone. In fact, she really liked a lot of them. She did not really understand any of them, though; she never had.

Then there were her parents. Now, talk about a lack of understanding. They were probably at the top of that list. She had petitioned them to allow her to drop out of school earlier that year. She did not go about it irresponsibly, of course. Before even broaching the subject, Jedda had drawn up an entire proposal with a very detailed plan of self-study. It included varied reading materials and exercises that she felt would help her achieve a well-rounded viewpoint of the world, a fine course of study for only the most diligent. She presented it to them with cheerful glee and a healthy dose of optimism. They didn't buy it. What was that irritating comment they made? Something about having a responsibility to help steer her away from doing things she might later regret. Blah blah blah. Were they even listening to her, or themselves, for that matter? This proposal was brilliant. Well, with all this walking down memory lane, Jedda definitely did not have time to go back to sleep.

Jedda started to arise from her bed when, suddenly, she began to recall that dream she was having just before waking. What was that about? It was kind of fuzzy now, all jumbled together. It seemed very otherworldly and quite difficult to think about now that she was really awake. There was a forest. It was different, though, somehow. It was not spooky or scary. It did have a strange feeling to it, though. It was what she imagined an enchanted forest to feel like. She let her romantic side get the best of her. It felt as if it were alive. Of course, all forests were alive, but this was unusual, like it was breathing, and you could feel it. She giggled at the thought. How do you feel something like a forest breathing anyway? How do you feel anything in a dream? She shrugged it off. Time to get ready for school.

Chapter 2
Ready or Not

"This place is a dream. Only a sleeper considers it real."

—Rumi

Maine – 2004

Jedda got ready the same way she always got ready: cold and by herself. Everyone in the house was either gone or sleeping. No big deal. She liked it quiet; it gave her time to mull over all the significant things of life: what test she had that week, what she was going to eat for breakfast, what the stars might look like from another planet. Whatever came to mind, really. This was her time. She also liked being the only one awake and moving about, because on cold days such as these, she could sneak over to the thermostat and crank that puppy up.

The warmth began to spread through the house. Now she could fathom the daunting process of undressing required if she intended to bathe. She chuckled to herself. Her parents still hadn't noticed a spike in the use of the electricity. What they didn't know wouldn't hurt them. Then a vision arose of the perplexed faces of her parents as they sat and gaped in disbelief upon opening an envelope with a hugely increased electric bill. A twinge of guilt arose. She waved it away. She was always sure to turn it back down just before leaving the house anyway. Besides, if they wanted to live in the Artic, they should join Santa Claus in the North Pole. She was sure he had enough room; the elves couldn't take up that much space.

Jedda loved the idea of the cold—it was crisp, cool, and refreshing. She just didn't like actually being cold. It felt like a cage. Like a bird, Jedda did not fare well in a cage.

The soothing hot water of the shower was revitalizing. Jedda loved the steam and heat that brought her back to life and the waking world. This was the final morning ritual necessary to shake off the remnants of the Sandman's work and be present to the day ahead. She reveled at the delightful warmth.

Something kept gnawing at the edges of her consciousness, though. What was it? While, normally, this was a time where she was without mind chatter, she could not shake the images from her dream. The Forest. And who was that woman dancing through the trees? It looked as if she had been extracting some sort of golden liquid from them. However, it was something about her interaction with the trees to which Jedda kept flashing back. The woman had been so loving, so reverent. It was like she was talking to them without words. How

Jedda knew this was beyond her, but she did know. The connection the trees and the woman shared was easily perceived. It was as if they loved one another. It was so strange and yet familiar, normal almost. Then there was that bird, she mused...

The water began to run cold. Jedda needed to get a move on it. She had spent way too much time pondering this dream. If she did not hurry, she was going to be late, and that was a road she did not want to go down today. She hopped out of the shower, dried off with her favorite green towel, and off she went.

Chapter 3
A Prepositional What?

*"When people begin to understand what they
are creating by their thoughts and their actions,
and their emotions, they will perhaps
understand the great need for discipline
in their lives."*

—White Eagle, *Spiritual Unfoldment Two*

Maine – 2004

While at school that day, Jedda was much less focused than usual. She began to daydream about that bird and all the magnificent colors of its feathers. What was bizarre was that in her dream, the bird appeared to be pure black like a raven or a crow. But now, as she allowed her mind to glide over it again and again, it began to change. She could see all these beautiful colors radiating out from it. As she tried to steady her concentration to focus on one color, it would morph into another vibrating hue: ruby red, velvet green, royal purple. Then her thoughts were jarringly interrupted.

"Jedda, would you like to tell us what you think? Hmm…" Mr. Ramen called on her. He apparently had noticed she was preoccupied.

What now? Couldn't he see she was in the middle of a perfectly exciting daydream? Mr. Ramen meant well, but he did have his quirks. That was why she liked him, though. One of his pet peeves was a student not paying attention in class. He liked structure and order. The rational mind and all its facets was Mr. Ramen's favorite topic. He loved to analyze and categorize. He should have been a mathematician, for goodness' sake, as there was no shortage of order there, although Jedda did not care for the subject very much. Alas, Mr. Ramen was an English teacher. He said there was plenty of order in the English language; one needed only to be willing to look for it. That was what sentence diagraming was for, and Mr. Ramen was a stickler when it came to that: one line under the subject, two lines under the predicate. "No, no! We do not box our direct objects; we draw a circle around them. The boxes are exclusively for indirect objects." What a headache! Mr. Ramen was passionate, though, to a fault. Jedda admired passion in anyone, even if it was about sentence structure.

"Could you repeat the question please? I am not sure I understood it completely," Jedda offered.

By the perturbed look on his face, it was clear that Mr. Ramen was not falling for her excuse. Jedda felt bad. She did not like upsetting Mr. Ramen. He was, after all, a very sensitive old man. He took it personally when someone was not paying attention, as if his teaching were to blame. He just did not quite understand that this subject was about as intriguing as counting the cracks in the sidewalk. It never failed, though. After all these years, he was still prone to getting his feelings hurt. How old was he anyway? He had to be at least a hundred, ventured Jedda, with that long white beard and glasses so large and thick they looked like two clear hockey pucks wired side by side. Rumors had it that he had been teaching for decades—no one really knew for sure.

In any case, she was not getting out of this one. "I'm sorry, Mr. Ramen. I must not have been paying attention."

There. She had said it. Cringe. *Get ready for it,* she told herself.

"Jedda, how many times have I explained how important this particular subject is? It will help you in all aspects of your life. Sentence diagraming can be applied to the nature of the universe," Mr. Ramen scolded.

"Yes, Mr. Ramen. You are right. I will do my best to focus. I was just a little tired, that's all. But I will make a valiant effort to push through." Jedda hoped he had not picked up on the hint of sarcasm in her voice. She did not mean it to be rude. She just had a difficult time placing such emphasis on diagramming the entire English language.

"Harold, could you tell us what we do with a prepositional phrase in this particular circumstance?" Mr. Ramen had moved on, thankfully.

Jedda was glad this was her last class. She was anxious to get home. Today was a wash, because she could not seem to stop thinking about that dream. Tomorrow would be a new day. She just needed to make it through another twenty minutes.

Chapter 4
Do You See What I See?

"Morning has broken, like the first morning,
Blackbird has spoken, like the first bird."

—Eleanor Fargeon, *"Morning Has Broken"*

Maine – 2004

Friday. The school week was finished. Finally. Jedda exited the bus at the corner of her neighborhood. This week had not been so bad. It did get off to a rocky start with that dream that had distracted her earlier in the week. She had hardly thought of it since then. It was only now, as she did a mental scan of the events of the last few days, that she drummed up the fuzzy recollection. It had really captivated her attention. It was fascinating, to say the least. Well, it was enough to have almost gotten her in trouble with Mr. Ramen. That was for sure.

She arranged her book bag and began the peaceful quarter-mile walk home. She enjoyed this part of the day. Jedda would take her time strolling along. She loved looking at the many diverse kinds of trees that lined the streets. There were pines, oaks, and a hemlock or two. Then there were the ones that flowered like the cherry tree and the crabapple. Of course, they were not in bloom just yet. It still felt pretty cold outside. March in Maine was not warm, and it certainly did not feel like spring even though the vernal equinox was just around the corner.

She rounded the last corner of her walk. At last, she had arrived on her street, Brook Lane. Her house was the third one down the winding path on the right. She could see the large willow tree that announced her home from here. How she loved that tree! Its bare-naked branches hung low and were swinging from a sudden gust of wind. It whipped by chilling her nose. Then it howled, as if taunting her.

The wind blew again: "Jedda…" a hiss was heard as it thrashed by. She stopped dead in her tracks. She turned around. There was no one there. It had sounded like someone had just whispered her name. Was she losing her mind? It must have been the sound of the wind whistling through the trees.

Jedda wrapped her wool coat around her more tightly and continued on down the hill. She was nearly approaching her front lawn when the wind blew again. It drew her attention to the willow tree as it rustled the branches with all its might. Then she saw it! She stared up into the branches in disbelief. She had not noticed it before now. Where did it come from? There, perched on the lowest branch of the willow tree, sat a strange black bird. The bird was staring right at her. If she did not know better, she would have thought it was watching her.

"Jeddaaaah...." There was that voice again. She whirled around. Again, there was no one there. She turned back. Only the black bird was there. Was the bird calling her? Impossible.

That was it! This was ridiculous! She must be delirious. Perhaps it was the lack of sleep that she had experienced this week that was now catching up to her. Maybe it was the amount of stress she was under to perform well in academics that she appalled. Jedda knew there was a breaking point. Perhaps she had reached it. She slowly advanced a couple of steps closer. The bird did not move. Suddenly, it let out a loud crow. Startled, she jumped nearly three feet high. The bird did not even flinch. It remained eerily still and fixated on her.

Now enough was enough. Was she really frightened of a black bird in broad daylight? She was clearly watching too many horror movies lately. She continued this staring contest with this winged creature of the night. What really started to disturb her was that she began to notice it had an unsettling resemblance to the bird in her dream from a few nights ago. She locked in on its eyes. They pierced right through her. She realized then that she was not actually afraid of the creature. It was mesmerizing, but not in a threatening way. She felt drawn to it. Then in that moment something happened. Something stirred within her. It felt like a flutter in her heart. An opening occurred. It was ancient and natural. It was terrifying, and then she heard the bird speak.

Chapter 5
A Wizard in Training

"Geometry existed before the creation. It is co-eternal with the mind of God...Geometry provided God with a model for the Creation..."

—Johannes Kepler

Moon Clan Community – 11,000 BCE

Taivyn jabbed his sword forward. Then he proceeded to jump and fling himself around as he swatted at what appeared to be a fly. Another jab here, then a strike. Swoosh! Around he went again, his sandy brown hair picking up as he spun. He looked more like a pirouetting ballerina than a swordsman. Thank goodness it had been a wooden sword, or he could have done some serious damage.

Taivyn Green was in training in one of the greatest Mystery Schools of all time. Well, maybe not the greatest Mystery School. The Atlantians had them beat for sure. The Egyptians probably surpassed them, too, but who could know. The Egyptians confused Taivyn with all their esoteric hoopla. They put the mystery in Mystery School. Then the Atlantians had to go and complicate things with all their numbers and geometric symbols.

No matter. Taivyn was just fine and content right where he was. After all, he was a wizard, and he was studying with a great master! Well, he was not exactly a wizard. He was more like a Keeper—in training, but he liked the sound of wizard better. It had a much more adventurous connotation to it.

Swish! The wooden sword-like staff went again. "En guarde!" Taivyn yelled in his most intimidating voice. It would have been hard to scare a grasshopper with that boyish screech.

Taivyn, who had just celebrated his sixteenth birthday, was rather tall for his age. He wore his height extremely well, though. He had a medium build with obvious definition that had resulted from all the labor-intensive chores he liked to do, including his work with the horses. There was something about those animals that he understood more so than the people around him, which made him feel awkward and different. However, the ladies didn't seem to mind his awkwardness a whole lot, as there was never a shortage of female attention anywhere he went.

"Taivyn! What are you doing!" a voice called emphatically from the distance.

He looked up as he hopped to his right and swung his wooden "sword" again. He could make out the Master's dark blue robes swirling in the gentle breeze as he approached from the Forest.

"I'm preparing to be a great wizard warrior!" Taivyn called out in answer to his obviously rhetorical question.

The elder rolled his eyes and scoffed. *Warrior. What nonsense!* he thought.

Master Ra-Ma'at was a tall and lanky man. He was by no means frail of either physical strength or character. He appeared to be in his late sixties, but those who were initiated knew him to be much older than that. He was coming into his 111th year, and all who celebrated the festival at the Spring Equinox would also honor and celebrate his birthday. Ra-Ma'at was a Solar Keeper of the Moon Clan. He had been initiated into the Mysteries long ago and was committed to keeping the ancient tradition alive. Honor the Beloved Creator who expresses as the Great Spirit within all life—the Divine Father/Mother Principle—that was what the sacred mystery teachings of his tradition taught.

Ra'Ma'at was finally close enough to see what Taivyn had been up to.

"Taivyn, how many times must I tell you that we, as a people, are not fighting warriors? You have misunderstood the metaphors that speak of a spiritual warrior. The only battle we do is with our own inner shadow. We expose our fears for the illusions that they are. Then our inner light can shine forth free of any impediment. It is then and only then that we can go forth in service to our brothers and sisters of the human race."

Ra-Ma'at continued moving methodically from one point to the next. "And we are not wizards! We are Keepers of the Moon Clan. We do not go around commanding and ordering the elements about. Nor do we bumble about like inept fools casting curses on everything we see that displeases us, or casting spells to attract anything we desire for that matter. Our purpose is to…"

Still waving the wooden object about, Taivyn finished the Master's sentence: "…to work in harmony with Nature for the highest good of all." Clearly, the boy had heard this speech a dozen times before.

The Master continued, "Yes, that's correct. We wish to be of service, and we collaborate with Mother Earth, with the Faerie, Devic, and Angelic Kingdoms—all—to manifest Divine Will here on Earth."

Ra-Ma'at had gotten a bit carried away with his explanation, as was the case when he became flustered. He looked over at Taivyn, who, at this point, was hopping around like he had a frog in his pants.

Shaking his head, Master Ra-Ma'at scolded, "It's a good thing you're not over there in Atlantis with Dr. Z. He'd never stand for this behavior."

Good thing, indeed, thought Taivyn. If he were in school in Atlantis, he would be required to study that Sacred Geometry. No way! Not Taivyn! All those numbers, lines, and angles did not make one bit of sense to him. He decided to question his teacher about this subject.

"Master Ra-Ma'at, what are all those lines and shapes supposed to tell you anyway? They are so abstract! Why can't they just make it simple like we do by teaching about the Earth and her elements? At least I can see that!" Taivyn complained.

Ra-Ma'at breathed a sign of exasperation. He had thought he had mastered the virtue of patience back in his earlier days. It just went to show that one is never quite finished being a student. *Just when you master one level, ten more open up and await you—each one deeper and more profound,* he mused to himself.

Ra-Ma'at began to breathe deeply. He did this to return his focus to the stillness within, thereby attempting to regain his composure. The boy did have a way of keeping him on his toes by pushing any remaining buttons he had. Still, he loved the boy dearly. Taivyn reminded him of himself when he was just a young lad filled with wonder and curiosity. Master Ra-Ma'at was still filled with wonder every time he beheld the natural world. Of course, his wonder and curiosity had not led him to impulsive and reckless behavior. Never mind. He had chosen to take on this pupil, and Taivyn would be the last one he would take through the sacred initiations—if Taivyn made it that far. Ra-Ma'at did have to wonder.

Master Ra-Ma'at was jolted back to the present moment when he heard an obnoxious grating sound. He turned to find Taivyn dragging the wooden sword-like object back and forth along the gate. Then, at once, he realized that was not just any wooden object. It was his staff!

"Taivyn! What are you doing? That staff is not meant to be a toy. It represents the great fire element."

"Really?" Taivyn responded, sounding confused. "But it's just a stick." With that he dropped it to the ground. You could hear the thump of it hitting the dirt.

21

Well, I've certainly got my work cut out for me, Ra-Ma'at thought. "What were we talking about before I realized you were misusing my staff?"

"You mean before you dazed off into the Summerlands?" Taivyn retorted sarcastically. The Master had been doing that a lot lately. What was going on with him? Normally, he was pleasant and playful, joyful and lighthearted. Lately, he had been slightly irritable and aloof, downtrodden even.

"All right! That's enough out of you…"

Taivyn quickly interrupted him, hoping to squirm out of being disciplined. "We were talking about the sacred shapes that the Atlantians teach about," he offered.

"Ah yes," Ra-Ma'at began to recall, stroking his long white beard ever so soothingly. He pulled himself up straight and cleared his throat: "Right, yes, but of course. Well, you see, my dear boy, all roads actually lead to the One. Nature is our road and the way we access the Divine, but there are many, many paths. If you look carefully at them all side by side, you will begin to notice many similarities. Eventually, you will realize they are all really the same. There is usually just a different way of expressing the same idea," Ra-Ma'at continued. "Different people see things differently. That is what makes us all so special. That is what makes life so rich."

Even though Taivyn was drawing circles in the field, he could tell that the boy was still listening, so he continued, "What we see as the elements of nature are expressed by the Atlantians in Sacred Geometry. You see, geometry is in nature, and nature is geometry. You cannot separate the two."

Taivyn's head started to spin. What was he talking about? Math in nature? Now he was sure the Master had lost a marble or two.

Master Ra-Ma'at went on. "In fact, each of the five basic geometrical forms represents one of the elements."

Now Taivyn was confounded. "But that would make five elements. I thought there were only four: earth, air, water, and fire?" Taivyn sat up confused.

Ra-Ma'at stared off in the distance as if recollecting something. "Ah yes, my boy. Well, you see, you still have much to learn. That lesson, however, is for another time. Come now. It's getting late. The community supper will soon be served. We must go to wash up."

Just then the sweet chiming bells began to ring in the distance, indicating that the time for meal was fast approaching. Taivyn jumped up and started to follow Master Ra-Ma'at, who had already turned to start back to the village. Then Taivyn paused. "Master Ra-Ma'at, how did you learn all of this stuff?" he asked in an uncharacteristically sincere way.

Master Ra-Ma'at stopped for a moment and then replied, "Taivyn, my boy, I listen to the trees as they tell their stories."

The Master let the boy ponder this for a moment and then continued, "And it is the Faeries who taught me how to hear and listen to the trees."

23

Chapter 6

Do You Hear What I Hear?
—An Unlikely Invitation

*"And I say unto you, Ask, and it shall be given
you; seek, and ye shall find; knock, and it shall
be opened unto you."*

—Luke 11:9

Maine – 2004

Jedda stood motionless while staring in disbelief. Try
as she might, she was unable to look away from the
crow-like bird. She wanted to run, but she could not
move. She felt frozen. What was happening? She must
be going mad. She was sure of it.

In a croaking voice, the large black bird continued,
"It's rather rude not to say anything in reply. I said,
'Good day to you, Jedda.' Won't you converse with me
for a while?"

"Heeelllloooo…" Jedda stammered. Although she
was not quite sure how she even managed that, seeing

as her throat seemed to have a rather massive lump growing with every moment. She gulped. She tried to breathe to calm herself, but it only made her heart race faster.

"Well, don't just stand there. You must be frozen to the bone. It is quite breezy in these parts. Won't you come inside for a cup o' tea?" the bird asked in a nasal voice much lower pitched than a mere crow.

Jedda had barely gotten over the fact that the bird was speaking to her. The invitation to "come inside" went almost completely over her head. As her attention came back to her body, she realized she was nearly an icicle; she was so cold. Then, slowly, she began to grasp what the bird had said. He was inviting her inside. Inside! Where, inside her house? *That would go over well with her parents*, she thought to herself. She had brought home enough stray animals to last her a lifetime. In fact, it was probably about three too many. She still was not completely off the hook from the last animal she had rescued and brought home—Artemis, her beautiful and gentle feline friend. She would never get away with bringing a wild bird inside. Besides, Artemis would have a field day with…

The bird interrupted her thoughts. "Won't you come inside?" the bird repeated as something began to materialize in the trunk of the willow tree. Jedda rubbed her eyes. Was that a door? It appeared to be forming out of thin air.

At this point, Jedda thought to herself, *I must be dreaming,* and with that she conceded. "How do I get in?" Jedda asked. It seemed like a reasonable question.

The bird said very matter-of-factly, "Why, you knock of course," followed by a loud and somewhat anxious crowing sound.

Jedda stood, looking curiously at the door. A doorknocker with a mysterious emblem had emerged on it. The emblem consisted of two circles overlapping one another, creating an oval intersection. Jedda studied it for a moment. She was sure she had seen that symbol elsewhere. She had no idea where, though. Jedda drew a deep breath in and held it for a second. As she let it out, she approached the door and grasped the handle of the knocker. She knocked three times and backed away. She waited. She wondered if she should knock again, so she stepped forward. Without warning, the door creaked open.

Jedda took another deep breath. Then she entered.

Chapter 7
A Cozy Space between Two Worlds

*"Faeries take us to a land where wisdom is
inseparable from whimsy, and where
Leprechauns dance with angels."*

—Brian Froud, *Good Faeries, Bad Faeries*

Willow Tree Cottage – 11,000 BCE

What Jedda found inside was not at all what she was expecting. She didn't know what she had expected, but it definitely was not this. As she looked around, she seemed to be inside some sort of tree cottage dwelling. The walls were made of vertical reddish-brown logs. The wood appeared rough and natural, not sanded down. There were crystal stalactites growing from the ceiling that mirrored back her reflection. Bright green leaves grew on vines that sprung up out of the walls. There was a rather large table just near her to the right that had an interesting array of things atop it: bird feathers, crystals, a candle, some herbs drying, some fresh cut flowers in the center, and a handful of other items that were not recognizable.

There was another room just up ahead. From where Jedda stood, she could see a fire blazing. The hearth was flanked by two upholstered chairs of a deep purple color sitting opposite one another and separated by a small table. Upon the small table was a pewter serving tray that held a simple blue-and-white glass teapot. Steam was coming out of the spout. In front of it was a matching teacup and saucer.

"Won't you come and sit down? Take a load off. Come now. Warm yourself by the fire with me. Have an endless cup of tea," squawked the bird.

Jedda was so engrossed in her new surroundings she had almost forgotten all about the talking bird. She walked over to sit down near the fire. The bird was resting on a wooden perch that looked like it had been made just for it. Things just kept getting stranger and stranger.

"An endless cup of tea?" Jedda inquired of the bird as she sat down and made herself comfortable. He motioned with his wing, indicating the teapot and teacup sitting on the small table.

"I was more specifically referring to your use of the word 'endless.'" Jedda attempted to clarify her question.

"Well, it doesn't have to be endless, if you don't want it to be," the bird answered, still not quite understanding. "Have a spot at least."

Jedda gave up trying to get a straight answer to what she believed to be a very obvious question. She lifted the teapot and began to pour the hot liquid into her cup. She filled her cup to the brim and then sat back. As she brought the teacup to her mouth to take her first welcome sip, she noticed it was green. She grimaced; she wasn't really in the mood for green tea, but it would have to do, she supposed.

As if reading her thoughts, the bird said, "If the green tea you don't fancy, just change it."

She looked up at the bird with one eyebrow raised. Before she could form a thought, the raven continued, "We are in a place where things aren't as…" The bird searched for the right words and went on. "…permanent," he finished, looking somewhat satisfied with himself.

Why did the bird have to be so complicated? If there was a cabinet that had other tea selections, why couldn't he just say so? She yielded to playing his game. "Okay, well, I'd like some herbal tea. Could you please tell me where to find it? Maybe it is in one of those cabinets in the other room. I could just get up and…"

He cut her off. "Everything you need is within you. You don't have to go anywhere to find it really. Herbal tea, huh? You need to be more specific with your desires."

Jedda was getting annoyed with the bird's cryptic language. "Sir, you don't have to be this difficult. You could just tell me where to find the other teas like peppermint or something besides…"

She trailed off because what happened next took her by complete surprise. Her tea instantly changed. The color shifted to a slightly darker shade that was no longer green, but a light brown color. The smell of peppermint greeted her nostrils.

"What just happened?" Jedda managed. "I think my tea just changed…to…peppermint…"

Staring at her intently, the bird stated, "Yes, well of course it did. That is what you asked for, isn't it? As I mentioned, we are in a sort of portal in between worlds. The laws of matter and physics that you are so accustomed to aren't as universal as one might think. In fact, everything works just a little differently here."

Jedda was preoccupied. She had raised her cup and was examining it underneath. Then her scrutiny moved to the saucer, turning it over and carefully looking it up and down. *What in the world is going on here?* she thought to herself. Still assessing the situation, she muttered more musing to herself than anyone else, "How did it do that?"

The bird waved it away, as if it were nothing. "By the way, I don't believe we've been properly introduced. I know you humans like naming things, people, animals—everything really. So you may call me Yuri. I am Yuri, the raven."

"Yuri? What an interesting name for a bird." Jedda stopped, suddenly realizing that her harmless comment could seem rude. She quickly added, "Well, I am pleased to formally meet you, Yuri. I'm Jedda, but then you already knew that, because you called my name out there. It wasn't the wind, was it? It was you."

"Yes, in a manner of speaking, it was. I wasn't actually talking as you do, but I was speaking to you." With that Jedda realized the raven wasn't really talking *now*. She could understand him all right, but his beak wasn't moving. She could hear him so clearly, though.

Yuri continued, "And yes, I did know your name. I was sent to you."

Sent to me? Jedda thought. *What on Earth does he mean?* Suddenly, she remembered the dream. She recalled the raven perched on a branch of that giant oak tree, watching.

"Yes, it was me you saw in the dream," Yuri confirmed.

Startled, Jedda gasped with surprise. "You know about the dream...? About the Forest...and the circle of trees...and that woman...?"

Although it wasn't a woman at all. Jedda knew that when she spoke the word aloud, it wasn't quite right. The being was too ethereal to be a human, and yet more tangible than she would have thought a ghost to seem. Then again what did she know about ghosts anyway. She became excited. She didn't know what any of this meant. She looked up at the raven, searching for some answer to questions she didn't even know how to begin to ask. As frantic as she was, she felt it slip away as if replaced by a warm blanket of serenity. She knew that Yuri was doing this. He was somehow calming her and making her feel comfortable again.

"What did you just do?" Jedda asked. Only the slightest tinge of agitation remained.

"What we can all do for one another if we wish to. Have you ever felt comforted while being out in nature, next to trees or beautiful flowers?"

Jedda thought about this for a moment. She fondly recalled hiking through the forest, touching the trees, sitting at the base of their large trunks, and daydreaming. Sometimes she even felt this love and peace when she was with animals. Her cat, Artemis, for instance, was her sweet companion. She loved it when he would jump up on her lap and circle around until he found the perfect spot. Then he would make a big production of stretching before nestling in her lap. Jedda loved listening to him purr as she stroked his black fur. She loved her cat. Yes, Jedda had definitely felt this peace and love before. She knew it well. She didn't know it could be something that one could consciously evoke, though.

"We can talk more about that later. For now I want to talk to you about why I have come," Yuri said, trying to steer them back on track.

Jedda began to contemplate the dream again. This time she felt peace as she allowed the images to flow. She definitely wanted to understand some of what she saw in the dream. She recalled the land and how it appeared moonstruck...

"That was you really seeing nature for the very first time. You saw it more clearly. What you saw was nature vibrating with life force energy. You thought the Forest was breathing; you were seeing the Forest tell its stories. Each creature and every living thing in the Forest has a story to tell. All perspectives are woven together to form the intricate and rich tapestry that is the story of Life. Each perception of reality flavors the One Reality in some way. That is how I see it anyway," said Yuri.

Chapter 8

Symbols and Scrolls and Elyrie—Oh My!

"I am the Light of Life within you and I have continued to shine through all the darkness of your manifold experiences, but your darkness has comprehended me not."

—Ruby Nelson, *The Door of Everything*

Moon Clan Community –11,000 BCE

He sat in the Tower, pouring over volumes of ancient texts. He had been spending a great deal of time intently scanning the scrolls and time-weathered documents. Many of the books were so worn one was almost hesitant to touch them. Their pages were yellowed and faded, their bindings thin and tattered. These works contained much of the Wisdom of the Ages. Their pages were filled with hermetic symbols, the magical history of the Earth (all but lost to the world today), and wisdom teachings from all over the world, both modern and ancient.

Master Ra-Ma'at had spent the last several days up there. He had hoped to find something that would shed some light on his most recent premonitions. He had started sensing something unusual weeks ago during the New Moon. He thought it was just a slight disturbance on the universal grid. "These things usually tend to iron themselves out, as everything eventually responds to the Universal Law of Balance," he assured himself, and so he didn't give it much thought beyond that at first.

Instead of the sensation "ironing out," though, it began to intensify. First, it would hit him out of nowhere, and then be gone. Now it had grown to a pervading feeling of dread. He started having dreams and visions that were leaving him uneasy. *She* was in many of them. Nothing was clear, though. They were more like momentary impressions that he could not quite grasp. One thing was for sure: he had not felt this before. No, this was different. Something was happening, shifting in some way. And something was definitely wrong. *If only she were here,* he thought to himself as a great sadness washed over him.

He had awoken again that morning with the same unsettling sense of foreboding. When his meditations didn't illuminate anything, he returned to the Tower once again. The Tower was the name the Moon Clan used to refer to the vast library of archives that had been collected over the centuries. It was quite separate from the main library. Although it was open to all of the initiates, only a handful of them dared to venture into this mysterious wing. Proper training was required just to handle some of the documents.

Master Ra-Ma'at was not only trained in caring for these works, he was adept when it came to deciphering cryptic texts. He had spent the earlier years of his life as a scribe for the Moon Clan. He used to transcribe many of the works to more durable materials so they would outlast the ages. Others had required translation, and so he had seen to that. He could read and write many of the ancient tongues: Sanskrit, Sumerian, Aramaic, Hebrew, and a dozen other languages that many did not even recognize by name. Although this work had been extremely laborious, Master Ra-Ma'at was grateful for it, for he had gained quite an understanding as a result of it.

As he continued to scan the myriad scrolls looking for some clue, he began to recall an ancient record he had come across long ago. At the time, the record had caught his attention because of its mysteriously mesmerizing effect. It had been recorded and stored within a large quartz crystal, as everyone knew that was the best and most accurate way of storing information. When he had placed his hand upon the crystal to access its records, it glistened and flashed light. It wasn't just the crystal that was shiny; the message itself was infused with this otherworldly glow. The message vibrated, as if calling him. It spoke directly to him, and yet he did not understand its meaning. Suddenly, images began to glide into his mind's eye like a stream of consciousness. He understood, and yet he did not understand. The symbols and images spoke to him at the deepest level of his being; however, his conscious mind could not make the jump. This had been his first encounter with Elyrie.

The Elyrie language was an ancient one—from the time of the Beginning some would say. Others spoke of it as a Language of Light, for it contained tones and sounds that came straight from the Great Oak and the first light seeding of the Earth. No one knew for sure. This language had been known and used throughout the lands in the ancient civilizations of Lemuria and Shambala and those even older, whose names had all but vanished from the lips and minds of men.

Although this mysterious first encounter had occurred when he was quite young, Master Ra-Ma'at had only endeavored to study Elyrie later in life. It was quite complex and enigmatic even for him. Yet somehow it was more natural than anything he had ever attempted in the past. He had never quite grasped this paradox. All was so clear when he had been with *her.* *She* had helped him a great deal as he delved into his studies of this ancient tongue, for she knew it well. It was, after all, the language of her people.

His mind wondered on, but then, it flashed once again to that puzzling record stored within the ridges of the crystal. How it had perplexed him with its mysterious reference! Master Ra-Ma'at tried to recount the words and images but found himself struggling. Somehow, he knew this ancient record held the key to something of significance for a time that had not yet come. Well, that time might very well be now, and, for some reason, he couldn't get his old noggin to cooperate. Drat!

Unfortunately, he would have to remember, because he did not have access to the crystal that contained that record. For it was no longer a part of the collection in the Tower, nor within the walls of their school. Nay. He had returned that crystal to its rightful place—the Crystal Library, which existed within *her* realm, one of the many places they had visited during their time together. *She* had taken him there as a gesture of love, knowing that the mere sight of the ageless collection would excite him beyond his senses.

Exasperated, he slammed the book that lay open before him shut! Master Ra-Ma'at collapsed on the long black oak table and breathed a final sigh of defeat. He felt hopelessness and despair begin to set in; he now became fully aware of the terror accumulating in this gut. His entire body was tense, bracing for something awful, and yet he had no frame of reference from which to identify it. He thought to himself about sending out an intention to call a Great Gathering and sighed again. For the first time in a very long time, he felt powerless, as if something very precious to him was about to slip away forever.

Chapter 9
The Council of Five

"He also forged her mystic mask out of the world's four elements (earth, air, fire, and water) melded with pure moonlight, the fifth element of Faery."

—Brian Froud, *Good Faeries, Bad Faeries*

The Great Gathering Place – 11,000 BCE

" . . . Awaken!"

In a clearing deep within the Forest, something was afoot. The birds chirped anxiously to one another, as a squirrel could be seen gathering his family into their home in a hole in the tree. A beaver was reporting what he had heard to a platypus. The frog was delaying his evening routine of song or croaking, depending on how one viewed it, while the mushroom had slipped away unseen. The frog pretended not to notice or care as he concealed a sigh of longing that rose up from deep within him. Anticipation filled the air.

Animals could be heard chattering amongst one another, while the insects were buzzing and fluttering about much more noisily than was typical at this twilight hour. Not one creature in the Forest was willing to miss an occasion such as this, for this event occurred rarely and only in the most crucial of circumstances.

There were others who waited, too (these other characters are not as easily understood in the world of Men, and yet they are pivotal to understanding the story of the Forest). Twinkling lights of various colors could be seen floating through the Forest canopy. Several Little People with pointed hats began to materialize out of the bark of the trees. Then the twinkling lights from up high began to descend from the tree tops; they hovered in midair.

Word throughout the Forest had spread quickly that the Council of Five had been called to convene, and all were waiting with expectancy to see if this would evolve into a Great Gathering. There were rumors, but no one knew for sure what the purpose of this meeting was. As the light grew less and the darkness set in ever so slightly, a strange phenomenon occurred. The veil between the worlds grew thin, and a different world started to emerge onto the scene. First, the light appeared to play tricks on the eyes as it did its last dance before allowing the shadows to engulf it. Slowly, one by one, five figures appeared as if out of thin air. Their white skin shimmered under the light of the waxing crescent moon, as if they were made out of stardust. There were both males and females among them, and they appeared regal like lords and ladies of a court without the frivolity. They each were unique in their own way characterized by a particular aspect or force of nature in which they governed. They were beautiful, and they were of the Faery Race.

Chapter 10
A Sunny Truth

*"Every blade of grass has its angel that bends
over it and whispers, 'Grow, grow.'*

—The Talmud

Willow Tree Cottage – 11,000 BCE

Lunaya sat upon a friendly rock that offered her respite underneath the shade of a great willow tree that was a part of her tiny cottage in the Forest. Following Sunny's suggestion, she had made a home upon the Polaris Ley Line, providing an easy way to locate her if a need should ever arise. Like a map, the ley line would lead them to where she dwelt. Additionally, the ley lines provided a very supportive work environment, as they were the energy meridians or pathways of the Earth.

Lunaya was beautiful and wise. Her appearance of timelessness made it difficult to guess her age. She had honey golden locks that bounded over her shoulders and spilled down her back like a river of golden light.

Her skin, a delicate milky white, was smooth and ageless. At times, she could appear thin and fragile; at others, her statuesque form betrayed the great power that she naturally commanded.

She listened to the sound of the stream running down the pebble-laden bed just in front of her cottage. Lately, it seemed to be in moments of silence like these that her feelings of nostalgia would invade her otherwise tranquil inner stillness. Clearly, she had felt confident about her chosen path, and she understood the consequences that her choice had entailed. Lately, however, she found herself reminiscing about the community.

Lunaya was a Moon Clan Keeper of the Highest Order. Her whole life had been spent learning to work in partnership with nature to promote balance and harmony; she thought of nature as the outer expression of the Divine. It was the part of Infinite Spirit that one could see, feel, touch, and even come to know. It was connection with the Divine that truly fed her soul.

She couldn't help but feel lonely at times, not having many on the physical plane with which to consort these days. Her time now was mostly spent wandering under the Forest canopy and listening to the stories of the animals, plants, and trees. She very clearly heard and understood the messages of the Forest. She might even speak to the Great Earth Mother if all the energies aligned to support a dialogue such as this.

Her life had become a realized dream, filled with miracles around every corner. She had indeed embarked on a wondrous journey. However, more and more Lunaya found herself desiring the comfort of community life. These were not so much feelings that stemmed from an unfulfilling life and great destiny; these emotions seemed to originate from a longing to be with her family, most especially her dear twin brother Sunny.

Lunaya's destiny had been carefully mapped and understood since birth. It had ultimately been her decision, though. She had chosen based on what she felt was best at the time. It had been a decision of duty, of responsibility. Lunaya knew and understood what it meant to commit to something. And commit she did. She had worked tirelessly all her life, but the importance of her work had definitely increased these last years.

She knew that her work to preserve the teachings was preparation for what lay ahead, for Lunaya understood well the cycles of time and the Turning of the Ages. Beginnings and endings of cycles always brought great changes with them, of course. But there was a magnified sense of urgency as of late, something she didn't quite understand, but she felt it in her center of power, at the pit of her stomach. Because of this, she knew it would only be a matter of time before a Great Gathering would be called. When that time came (and she would know, because those who were called could feel the invitation within their heart), she would hopefully have some answers that might help them know how to proceed.

The golden sun was setting, as it made its daily journey across the firmament. The remaining light colored the sky in a beautifully surreal way. Pink light painted its way across the azure canvas that was a vision for the eye to behold. Fire orange speckles danced around, creating what appeared to be a thousand tiny flints that had been sparked by some unseen hand.

It was skies like this that reminded her of her brother whom she missed above all else. They used to sit together and chat as the sun was leaving the sky. They had been so deeply connected all throughout childhood and even through their studies. They took their initiations in the Tree Mysteries together. The Tree Mysteries were part of the body of knowledge known as the Faery Wisdom Teachings; it was the highest and purest path one could take.

How she missed Sunny. Lunaya smiled. That had been her nickname for him. It was an inside joke between the two of them. Part of his real name was a reflection of his work as a Solar Keeper, for the ancient sun god was known as Ra.

Lunaya sighed. Perhaps for the feelings of solitude that colored her reality on days like this, or perhaps she intuitively sensed the dark inevitable, an event that would color the next 13,000-year cycle. In either case, it was getting late, and it was time to see if the raven had succeeded in his mission.

Chapter 11
Back to Life, Back to Reality?

"No man can reveal to you aught but that which already lies half asleep in the dawning of your knowledge."

—Kahlil Gibran, *The Prophet*

Maine – 2004

Jedda heard a familiar voice calling her name. It sounded muted in the background, as if it were reaching to her from across time and space. She had a sensation of being stirred out of a dream.

"Jedda!" the voice called again. She tried to get her bearings and steady herself. Everything seemed to be a blur at first. Jedda used all her willpower and concentration to focus on the reality before her. Then she realized where she was.

"Jedda Rose! Would you please come and help us with the groceries? There's a lot of bags, and we could sure use an extra hand."

The addition of Jedda's middle name was an indication of her mother's growing impatience. Diane Delaney was standing in the driveway next to Jedda's younger brother. They were lifting grocery bags out of the trunk. Apparently, they had just gotten back from the supermarket.

She looked around. She gazed at the willow tree. What had happened? A second ago, she was talking to a raven inside the tree. At least she thought she had gone inside the willow tree. Once inside, it did feel like she had entered a forest cottage or something. Now she was standing on the front yard of her house with the tree facing her. Had she imagined the whole thing? It had felt so real.

"Yeah, Jedda! Come help us!"

Well, that was enough to bring her back into the current moment. Boy, did her brother know how to push her buttons.

"Shut up, Jake!" she quickly retorted. Irritated, she started toward the car to offer her help.

It didn't take very long to get the groceries unloaded and brought up into the kitchen. Jedda made her way out the front door and back down to the car one last time for the remaining two bags. She lifted them out, set them on the ground for a moment, and slammed the trunk shut. As she bent down to retrieve the bags, she heard a faint whisper behind her that sounded like the wind whispering her name again. Familiar with this game, she whirled around, half expecting to see the raven. Nothing was there. She couldn't help but feel a little dismayed. She had hoped that what she believed to have happened with the raven was actually real. It sure would have been a refreshing twist to her usually boring and uneventful life.

Jedda sighed. She turned to grab the bags and started to walk inside. Disheartened, she made her way up the driveway. As she approached her front steps, something caught her attention. Out of the corner of her eye, Jedda saw something black and shiny flutter downward. Her stomach did a somersault. It landed on the ground next to her feet. She smiled to herself. A black feather.

Chapter 12
Mission Mode

"By learning more about the myths and magical beliefs of cultures all around the world...we gain a deeper understanding of the faery world around us today—particularly since faeries communicate to us through the use of mythic symbols, expecting that we (like our ancestors) will understand what they mean."

—Brian Froud, *Good Faeries, Bad Faeries*

Maine – 2004

Diane, Jedda's mother, was putting the groceries away in the fridge as Jedda hastily dropped off the two bags she had carried inside on the kitchen floor. Her mother raised an eyebrow as Jedda brushed passed her as inconspicuously as possible. She strode down the hallway and made a beeline for her room. None too quickly, for Jake appeared from around the corner, waving something in her face. He was trying to taunt her with something he had apparently taken from her room. Any other day, this might have sent her over the edge. Not today. Today, Jedda was on a mission, and this mission was much more important than dealing with her annoying little brother.

Jake sat stunned with bewilderment, as the door to Jedda's room slammed shut in his face. He was a little disappointed that his ploy had not gotten the slightest rise out of his sister. Something was definitely amiss, and he was determined to find out what it was. He turned to go back to his room to regroup. Then he thought twice about it, and instead turned back around and placed his ear up to her door and waited.

Jedda was pacing back and forth. Sometimes she did her best thinking in this manner. Her thoughts were racing, though. What had happened to her? She began rummaging around in her room for her journal. She wasn't in the mood to write, but she needed to recount an entry she had made earlier in the week. She checked her three usual hiding places: underneath her mattress, on top of the highest shelf in her closet, and her bookcase where it would blend in with the hundreds of other books that sat upon it. All to no avail. Drat! The little brat! That must've been what Jake had been flashing in front of her. Her temperature began to boil, and her cheeks flushed red. If steam could have come out, it would have been because she was seething pissed. "Get a hold of yourself!" she said out loud.

Unbeknownst to her, the thief sat perched outside her door, listening. A twisted smile crept across his face. He knew she was just now coming to the realization of what he had taken from her. Judging from the chaotic rummaging and the anger in her voice as she screamed and then scolded herself out loud, he knew he had struck more than a little nerve. Her journal must contain something juicy. More importantly, he now knew with certainty that it held within it something that might allude to her strange behavior. Satisfied with his plunder, Jake slid away unnoticed and returned to the safety of his room.

Jedda breathed deeply, trying to calm herself down. She would have to do without the entry and recount the dream from memory. She definitely didn't have time for Jake's antics right now. There were much more critical matters that needed attention. She sat down to think. She began to go over her conversation with the raven in her head. What in the world did she agree to?

Before she could think clearly about all that they had spoken of, there was something else. Something was poking and tugging on her, trying to get her to remember. What was it? Yes. She began to recall the image of that symbol that adorned the doorway she had supposedly walked through into the tree. It was two circles overlapping. Where they overlapped, an oval shape was created. What was this symbol? Jedda knew she had seen it somewhere before, but where?

Jedda got up and stood before her bookshelf. She began to hastily scan all the titles for some indication of what she was searching for. She knew that among these volumes and volumes of books, one of them had to provide some clue or insight as to the significance of that symbol. She pulled several off the shelves that she thought might be helpful and started to thumb through them.

With no luck yet, she quickened her pace. She was possessed by the drive to find something, anything at all. To an observer, she might have appeared slightly mad. For Jedda, though, this intensity was semi-normal when she was in mission mode. She had a target in sight, and she wouldn't rest until she found it. Besides, being so absorbed meant being able to avoid the inevitable—that she had to very carefully consider if she believed what she had just experienced was really reality, and if it was…well, then, she would have to consider the last thing she remembered the raven had said to her.

She brushed her hair out of her face, as she often did when she was trying to get serious. With it, she pushed any nagging thoughts about talking birds and agreements to the side as well. She needed to concentrate. Determined to find any shred of information, she pressed on, skimming page after page, book after book. Just when she was about to give up, she came across some interesting images. She felt goose bumps on her skin—a sudden ray of hope. Finally, something that might be of use.

It was in reference to Sacred Geometry, a subject that fascinated Jedda. However, she never could quite grasp its meaning because of all the complicated math that seemed to be involved in its explanation. There were pictures, though, and pictures she could understand. She liked to think of herself as a visual learner mostly. The page had several shapes on it. One of which appeared to be that same symbol. They called it a vesica piscis.

Below the image, it read: "The **vesica piscis** is a geometrical shape that is the intersection of two circles with the same radius, intersecting in such a way that the center of each circle lies on the perimeter of the other."

Well, that was obvious. She could see that. But what did it mean? How did it fit into everything that had happened? She knew it was somehow important. She had that feeling within telling her so. She scanned further down. The passage began going on about numbers and calculations. She could feel herself losing concentration, which often started to happen when she was on overload. Well, it didn't seem like this book was going to give her much else she could work with. The phrase "does not compute" seemed to play over and over in her head. Oh, well, at least she had confirmed that the symbol did exist; it wasn't just some figment of her imagination. She would have to place that in the "to be continued" file of her brain and carry on.

Now for the scary part. Right, the talking bird. Yikes. She thought back over everything the raven had told her. He had known so much about her, or at least enough to be enticing. The raven had said that to find the answers she was seeking, she would have to journey within. When she was ready to remember, she should return to the Forest. It was to this that she had agreed before leaving the willow tree.

Chapter 13
A Messenger Returns

*"Like Hermes with his winged sandals, the
faeries are fleet-footed communicators, bringing
us messages from the depths inside ourselves
and from the cosmos."*

—Brian Froud, *Good Faeries, Bad Faeries*

Willow Tree Cottage – 11,000 BCE

The raven was resting comfortably on his stoop near the fire inside the main room of the willow tree cottage. He appeared to be *between the worlds* now, as one could distinguish the audible drone that arose from his energy field when he was in this state of consciousness. Lunaya would never get used to that sound. It was a buzzing that not only could be heard but could be felt from within as a haunting vibration. She thought to summon him back to this time and place, but then decided against it. He was, after all, not known as The Messenger for nothing, for he alone had the unrivaled ability to move through the various realms of existence, the inner planes of light and beyond.

Yuri served the way of Great Spirit as he called the universal energy of the Divine. Specifically, the raven had been working with Lunaya under the guide and tutelage of the Ancient Ones. Lunaya knew that his spirit was with the Faery Ones now. She became excited, for that meant he had found something so significant that he was compelled to share the message with them first.

Lunaya walked over to sit down in the chair next to him to await his "return." She was just beginning to relax into the cushion when she noticed a half-drunk cup of tea sitting on the round table. She picked it up. The perplexed look on her face must have indicated her shock as a voice grabbed her attention.

"Something wrong?" asked Yuri sleepily. He had unnoticeably finished his journey between the worlds.

Somewhat startled by his abrupt entry back into her reality, she stammered, "Huh?" and then she quickly focused, "No, it's just that this cup of tea is slightly warm, and clearly I haven't had any. So I was wondering if, suddenly, you developed a fondness for the drink that I wasn't aware of, or if someone else has been here." Lunaya wasn't quite sure which explanation was more ridiculous.

She waved it away in an effort to table the conversation for later. After all, there were much more pressing concerns at hand than the raven drinking a cup of tea. Lunaya continued, "Anyway, enough about that. You can tell me all about your new interest in the fine drink later. Were you able to locate the Keepers?" she asked excitedly.

Yuri studied Lunaya's expression for a moment. He was clearly calculating exactly how to frame the next bit of what he was going to say. Forgoing the strategically planned explanation, he blurted out, "Not quite." With that he could feel a twinge of edginess begin to overshadow her excitement.

The raven thought about his next response for a moment before continuing his reply. He did, of course, understand how important the mission had been, or was. He knew she may want him to return and try again. Based on his findings, however, next time around, his mission might have a slightly different focus. For now, however, his discovery alone would have to suffice.

"What do you mean exactly?" Lunaya was definitely annoyed, but her curiosity had been piqued. There was a cryptic twinkle in Yuri's eyes. And for a second, Lunaya could have sworn she saw the bird smile.

The raven relaxed a bit as he nestled more deeply on his perch. He finally continued, "I believe I may've found something even better."

Chapter 14
A Plan of Action

*"Until the heart opens with courage the temple
door is barred. The muse waits for the strong
heart, to give the right mind."*

—Bhagavad Gita

Maine – 2004

Jedda thought about her conversation with the raven
again. She wasn't sure if she were ready to embark
on some journey of "remembering," as he called it. He
made it sound so…serious.

No, she definitely was not really ready to give it her
full attention just yet. She pushed the thought of it out
of her mind for now. She swiftly turned her focus back
to the symbol. Jedda just wasn't able to shake the inner
knowing that the symbol—what was it called again?—
right, the vesica piscis, was key to gaining a more
complete understanding to what was going on.
Somehow, she just *knew* that it was significant, maybe
even central.

Based on the little bit of rather vague information she had already unearthed, Jedda knew only one person who might be able to shed some light on that obscure and, according to that esoteric book, geometric form— Lou Silverton.

Her history teacher, Miss Silverton, was always directing the students' attention to symbols. She explained that art, architecture, and literature throughout history were encoded with information in the form of symbols. The symbols were like clues left behind that told stories. One had to learn to read the symbols to understand the story they were trying to tell. Miss Silverton felt that history could be better understood when taking all this into account. She said that solely relying on the written documentation that survived over the centuries was not always an accurate and well-rounded way to understanding past situations.

Now Jedda just needed to think about a brilliant foolproof approach. She needed some way to raise as little suspicion as possible. She was certainly not willing to share her experiences of the last week with anyone. They would have her committed for sure. She knew Miss Silverton to be somewhat open, and even unusual. Nevertheless, she could not chance it. Besides, this situation with the talking raven took things to a whole new level. Darn it! There was that part of the day's events that she would rather not dwell on right now.

All right! Enough! She had to think. What could she say? Then, suddenly, an idea came to her. She would tell Miss Silverton that she was doing a research project on various symbols. That was it! Yes, and she was interested in including this symbol in her preliminary research, because the lack of information pertaining to it caught her attention and intrigued her. Yes, that was good. It seemed like a sound plan. If all went accordingly, her history teacher would just give her what she needed without asking a whole lot of unwelcome questions. After all, wasn't this what all teachers ultimately wanted: for their students to be engaged in their subjects and interested in learning more?

With her plan contrived, all Jedda had to do was exhibit a little bit of forbearance; it was only 8:00 p.m. on Friday night, and Jedda would have to wait until Monday to execute her plan. "Great!" Jedda griped aloud. After all, patience was her least favorite of all the virtues. For the first time, she was looking forward to Monday morning with eager anticipation.

Chapter 15
What Dreams May Come

"The fairies went from the world, dear,
Because men's hearts grew cold:
And only the eyes of children see
What is hidden from the old."

—Kathleen Foyle

A tiny soft bluish light flickered in the night. The dew gave off a shimmering glow against the light of the moon. Somewhere in the distance, the gurgling of a babbling brook was audible as it made its way through the glen at the edge of the Forest. A frog was just beginning his twilight serenade, and a mushroom peaked out from under a leaf where light rain droplets made a pitter-pattering sound just overhead. The tiny light flickered again as it floated with intended purpose a few feet ahead.

Then there were two tiny twinkling lights. To and fro they danced as if to some unheard song. Perhaps they danced to the ballad the frog sang for the mushroom for *the first time in several millennia. Perhaps they danced to something else.*

The tiny lights could have been mistaken for fireflies if one did not take special care to notice. One possessing a sharp eye would not be fooled, however. For an astute one would clearly recognize the pastel colors of pink and powder blue that emanated from these tiny orbs, quickly distinguishing them from any known lightning bug. The Night Forest's song continued on, and the tiny lights continued floating in rhythm to this sweet otherworldly melody all too keen for most humans to hear; but "those with ears to hear" could perceive the intoxicating sound of strumming harp strings and wild wind chimes reverberating off lily pads and being carried by the mist. In perfect synch, a spellbinding liquid voice rose up as if from everywhere and nowhere all at the same time.

Then, as suddenly as the music had commenced, all became reverently silent, as if in some gesture that said, "Awaken…!"

Maine – 2004

Monday's arrival couldn't have been more painstakingly slow. What agony it had been to wait so long. Normally, weekends whisked by in the blink of an eye. Not this weekend. Jedda was beginning to believe in the concept of time being relative and definitely not a constant variable. Perhaps time was some mechanism put in place by whatever greater intelligence existed in the universe to taunt humankind. Well, it was definitely working. If God was some old man with a beard sitting on a throne in the clouds, he sure was getting more than his fair share of belly laughs. Jedda had an image in her mind that looked more like Santa Claus in the sky than some omnipotent Godhead. This image conflicted greatly, however, with what she felt when she was somewhere in nature. It was in natural places filled with trees and plants that Jedda felt the sacredness of life. Her heart would sing in joyful bliss, for she felt connected to all life everywhere. That was when Jedda was sure God was a woman, because, synonymous with a mother's love, Jedda felt comforted and nurtured.

These were her mind's wanderings as she sat quietly in the passenger seat of her mother's car. Jedda had missed the bus. By the time the next one would have come, she would have been seriously late for school. Jedda had slept through her alarm clock. This was ironically humorous considering Jedda had been so anxious all weekend for Monday morning to come. It wasn't really that funny, though, when her mother had glared at her so intensely that she thought she was going to bore a hole in her head. No, Diane had definitely not been thrilled to hear that she would have to drive her daughter to school that day.

Being late this morning wasn't entirely Jedda's fault; she had had the dream again—although she couldn't really explain that to her mom. Besides, this silent drive gave Jedda time to contemplate it all. Although it had been an intended show of distaste for her behavior, the silent treatment given by her mother had turned out to be a blessing in disguise. Had she ridden the bus, she would have never gotten a moment of quiet to analyze this new piece to the ever-unfolding puzzle.

The dream seemed to have some of the same elements as last time, but the emphasis was entirely different. This time Jedda had really felt as if she were actually there. She could feel a deep and inexplicable connection with that Forest; it felt as if it were a part of her. She saw that woman again. The woman wasn't doing anything specific; this time she had just been sitting among the trees in the Forest. There were several blue and pink orbs of swirling light glowing slightly above the woman. Jedda hadn't noticed these last time either. The woman, who was most certainly the focus of this dream, looked as if she were watching them with great attention. Who was she? In the dream she felt like she had known her. Now, as she allowed the images to flow, a strange sense of familiarity began to come over her again. Why did that woman seem so familiar?

Next, Jedda's attention was taken to the giant tree. There was a feeling of profound love for that tree that Jedda couldn't understand or explain even to herself.

Then there was that bird again, the raven. What did he say his name was? Jedda thought for a moment. Yuri. He had been sitting perched up high upon one of the branches of that oak tree in the center of the circle. He looked as if he were observing everything. Then something startling happened. He looked right at her. In that moment, the lines between dream and reality blurred. She was conscious of herself dreaming, yet she had not woken up. Then she caught a glimmer in the raven's eyes. If she hadn't known better, she'd have sworn the bird was smiling.

She heard the emphatic word, "Remember!" whispered imploringly. Whether it was coming from everywhere or within, she wasn't sure. That was the last thing she recalled. The dream had ended abruptly to the jarring sound of her mother yelling—an obvious indication that she had overslept.

The car came to a stop at the front entrance of her school. Her mother, apparently feeling a little remorseful about overreacting this morning, looked over at Jedda and smiled. "All right honey. I'm sorry I yelled at you this morning. You know how I get sometimes. I just wish you'd be a little more responsible and considerate. You know it's not that I mind driving you once in a while. It's just that it makes me late if we don't plan for it. Have a good day at school. See you when you get home."

Jedda smiled. She knew it was her mother's attempt at making amends before they parted for the day. "It's okay, Mom. I'm sorry, too. Bye. I love you."

Jedda shut the car door behind her and waved good-bye to her mother. Her mom waved back and drove off. Jedda started for the entrance just as the tardy bell started ringing. She rolled her eyes. What else was new? She continued on with one thought and one thought only: "All you have to do is make it to lunch. Then find Miss Silverton."

Chapter 16
Off to See the Wizard

"Myths and symbols are the carriers of meaning. In them, a situation is presented metaphorically in a language of image, emotion, and symbol. Because humans share a collective unconscious...a symbol comes from and resonates with the deeper layers of the human psyche."

—Jean Shinoda Bolen, *Like a Tree*

Maine – 2004

J edda knew Miss Silverton took her lunch the same time she did, because she often saw her in the library or teacher's lounge. She could have waited until sixth period when she had class with her, but the suspense would have killed her. No, Jedda had to take the first opportunity she got to ask her teacher about the enigmatic symbol. The rest would be history.

The morning dragged on. Jedda had not even had the slightest idea what any of her teachers had talked about all day. With her mind elsewhere, her lessons had been a daze. Over and over again, she played through the anticipated conversation with Miss Silverton in her head: exactly what she was going to say, how she was going to phrase it, what questions she would ask, how Miss Silverton might reply to her questions. She was getting more and more nervous. What was she so worried about anyway? She was simply asking for further information on a geometric symbol, which happened to be of great interest to Miss Silverton. It was quite possible that Miss Silverton wouldn't even know what in the world that symbol meant either, and if that turned out to be the case...well, then, she was back to square one. The bell rang, signifying the end of third period, and, along with it, the commencing of Jedda's lunch. She could not seem to scramble out of her seat fast enough.

Now, she had to find Miss Silverton, and fast. Jedda exited the classroom and walked through the hallway. Her first stop would be the teacher's lounge, which was on the first floor. She went through the east doorway that led to one of the many staircases and began her descent. With each step, her palms grew a little sweatier. Her mouth became dry, like she was chewing on a cotton ball. A tickle began to develop in the back of her throat.

All right! Knock it off! She scolded herself, *You have to remain calm. You don't want Miss Silverton to think she's talking with a basket case, do you? I didn't think so. Now pull yourself together.*

With that last line of pep talk, she reached the bottom of the stairwell. She paused for a moment before pushing forward. Then she spotted a bathroom at the other end of the hallway directly across from the teacher's lounge. She made a dash for it and slid in. She walked into one of the stalls just in case. If anyone were to come in, at least they would not witness her being weird. She sat down and closed her eyes. She tried to use her breathing to calm herself. Funny thing was it only seemed to work when she was already calm. Rats! She breathed deeply into her belly, just like she'd learned in yoga class. Then she exhaled forcefully, letting it all go. She continued to tell herself that there was nothing to be worried about. She walked out of the stall, over to the sink, and splashed some water on her face. She peered into the mirror. Jedda looked peaked. She hated how she always lost her color when she got anxious. It was like plastering a big sign on her forehead that screamed, "Nervous wreck on display!"

Jedda glanced at her watch. She only had another thirty minutes of her lunch period left. She needed to get on with it. It was now or never.

She bounded through the bathroom door with all the courage she could muster, and made her way over to the teacher's lounge. She paused at the door long enough to catch her breath and then knocked. Someone answered from behind the door, inviting her inside. She walked through, startled to find Miss Silverton standing right there. Wearing her hair in her usual way, her blonde curls hung loosely over her shoulders. Upon her thin frame, she wore a modestly long blue skirt and a cream-colored blouse. A turquoise stone necklace dangled from her neck. Her thin frame glasses were a perfect match for the fragility of her form.

By the looks of it, she appeared to be getting ready to leave. She was gathering her books and putting them in that funny looking satchel that she carried around with her everywhere. The bag looked ancient. It was bluish purple in color and was ripped a little on one side. The other side had a small hole in it, where the seam was coming unraveled.

Miss Silverton hoisted the satchel onto her shoulder. As she did, the other side came into view. Jedda gaped in disbelief. Never had anyone looked as stunned as Jedda did in that moment. There, sewn onto the satchel, was an emblem. It was as if the whole universe were playing some joke on her right now, which she did not seem to find very funny. In fact, she was downright befuddled. There, on Miss Silverton's satchel, for the entire world to see, was the vesica piscis. Jedda must have still been gawking and looking white as a ghost, because Miss Silverton suddenly stopped what she was doing.

In a concerned tone, she asked, "Jedda, is everything all right, dear? Are you okay?"

Shaken from her bewilderment, Jedda quickly managed, "Oh…um…yes. I'm fine. I just…uh…came to talk with you actually. Were you getting ready to leave?"

Miss Silverton was definitely intrigued. "You came to talk with me? Oh, well, wonderful. What can I help you with, dear?"

Jedda tried to spit out all the preplanned questions, but nothing was coming out. She sounded like a Neanderthal, "Oh, um...yes, well...I was coming to talk to you about...I wanted to ask you..."

Miss Silverton, picking up on Jedda's need to talk but also intuiting that this might not be the right place to do so, offered, "Jedda, I was just getting ready to go to the library. I assume you are on lunch right now and not cutting class?"

When Jedda's nod confirmed that, Miss Silverton continued, "Well, if you'd like to accompany me, we can continue this conversation, and you can ask me whatever it is that you came here for. Does that sound okay?"

Jedda breathed a sigh of relief. She hadn't even realized how the bright lights and surrounding teachers in the teacher's lounge had been contributing to her level of discomfort. She silently praised Miss Silverton for picking up on this. "That sounds great. Thank you," Jedda answered.

As soon as they exited the teacher's lounge, Jedda could feel the muscles in her body immediately begin to relax. It was incredible how unbelievably tense she had been. They began their stroll to the library located all the way on the other side of the building. Jedda started to feel much more comfortable. It was like Miss Silverton's presence alone soothed her soul. She loved Miss Silverton; she always had. Now, she could tangibly understand why. The woman was like an angel who seemed to know what she was feeling. Jedda smiled. Miss Silverton, sensing that Jedda had calmed down, started up the conversation again. "So, Jedda, tell me now. To what do I owe the pleasure of your visit today?"

Jedda felt safe, and, for some reason, began to open up a little more than she had expected, "Well, I came because I wanted to ask you about the meaning of a symbol that I came across the other day."

Without even realizing it, Jedda had completely forgone the little story that she had originally devised about the make-believe project. Without hesitation, she continued, "In fact, what's strange about the whole thing is that the very symbol that I was coming to ask you about is actually the emblem on your bag. I think it's called the…"

Before the words could come out of her mouth, Miss Silverton finished, "The vesica piscis. Yes. One of the most profound and ancient symbols in the world. But tell me, why does it suddenly interest you? How did it come to you?"

How did it come to her? Jedda thought that was an interesting choice of words. Jedda thought for a moment about how she wanted to answer Miss Silverton's question. Then she replied, "Well, I know this sounds strange, but I think I dreamt about it."

Just then Jedda realized a few things: first, she sort of just lied to Miss Silverton; second, somewhere in her mind, she had thought it was a good idea to share she was having dreams and that she gave value to them.

Just as she was about to start kicking herself, she heard Miss Silverton's gentle and reassuring voice, "Really? Well, that's wonderful, dear."

Surprised and relieved all at the same time, Jedda perked up, anxious to hear what Miss Silverton had to say.

"Jedda, this symbol is a wonderful symbol. Although you may think I know about this symbol from my interest in history, that is not quite the whole picture. You see, this symbol, and some others, are ancient and are part of what is known as Sacred Geometry. Symbols are important because they speak to our subconscious minds, and they usually have many layers of meaning. We used to understand the language of symbols. However, much of this wisdom has been lost. Fortunately, there are still those who keep this stream of knowledge alive. And I would like to tell you about the deep and intricate meaning of the vesica piscis, the symbol that has been presenting itself to you. Unfortunately, we have run out of time."

Jedda realized the bell was ringing again. That damn bell! It seemed to come at some of the most inopportune times. Jedda got panicky for a second; she feared that she had missed her chance to learn about the symbol.

However, Miss Silverton quickly dispelled Jedda's worries when she added, "Now, I would really like to share more with you about this topic, if you wish, of course. Do you perhaps have a day this week when you could come by my house after school? It really is a topic we should discuss without any outside distractions around."

Jedda was ecstatic. Could she come to Miss Silverton's house after school to learn about seemingly magical symbols? Was that a rhetorical question? She went through her schedule in her head...nope, nothing more important going on than this. Tuesday was the soonest she could agree to since she might have to inform her mother that she would not be coming home right after school. Yes, tomorrow would be perfect.

Miss Silverton continued with instructions. "You can ride the 222 bus over to Mayfair Park. My house is on the same street as the north side entrance; the address is 1300, and it's the white one with the red shutters and a red door. I should be there shortly afterward. We can have a snack and some tea. I will drive you home when we are finished. You're sure your mother won't have a problem with this, right?" Jedda shook her head that she wouldn't.

"Okay. Tomorrow it is then. See you in sixth period," Miss Silverton ended. She started to walk away.

Remembering something, Jedda quickly ran after her. "Miss Silverton, wait up. I was wondering how in the world could I not have remembered or noticed that the symbol, the...er..." Jedda struggled with the pronunciation. "...the vesica piscis was on your satchel?"

Miss Silverton smiled. "Jedda, sometimes we don't really see things until we are ready to see them. Ever heard the phrase 'hidden in plain sight'? Rest assured that things, people, places always come to us at the right and perfect times in our lives. We need only have 'eyes to see and ears to hear.'"

That sounded awfully familiar. Where Jedda had heard it before, she had no idea. The way things were going, she would just add it to the list of unsolved mysteries. Jedda smiled and did an inside leap of joy. She could not believe her good fortune. For once, luck was on her side, and life was finally getting interesting!

Chapter 17

A Light at the End
of a Keeper's Tunnel

*"The light of love illuminates all things,
transforms all things, and brings us closer
to a New Earth."*

—Thea Summer Deer,
Wisdom of the Plant Devas

Maine – 2004

Lou Silverton left school that afternoon right after last period. What was happening was incredible. She had never been so forthcoming with information the way she had been with Jedda earlier. Her intuition, which she relied heavily on, had told her it had been the right course of action. She could feel it. She knew it in her bones, and yet she could not help but feel a hint of nervous tension. She had waited so long for this. Never had she imagined it would happen in this way, though. She hadn't even suspected it could be connected with one of her students, academic students that is. She had actually thought it might be one of her apprentices who would eventually show the signs of readiness.

She had been teaching for half of her life now, and not just history. Lou had carried on the sacred teachings of her ancestors. Obviously, many of her apprentices showed promise, but in all this time, they didn't demonstrate the one thing she had been looking for. Actually, she didn't know what it was she had been looking for exactly. It was never really explained to her. Her teacher, who had been her aunt, had just said that when she found the one, she would know him or her. She had been instructed to keep her inner sight open and clear, and she would "see" them by the energy they exuded. But she hadn't seen anything. Until now. She was sure that Jedda was that one.

Lou walked through the front door of her little house. She went over to the couch to relax a bit and think. She would have much to do in preparation for her visit with Jedda the following day. Her mind started racing again. Then she heard a familiar sound.

Lou responded, "Hello, my sweet. And how have you been today? Well, you won't believe what has taken place."

Isis jumped up on the sofa, eager to procure a perfect spot in Lou's lap. She crawled on top, stretched, and landed.

"It looks like someone's sleepy," Lou continued.

The only response that she received was a soft meow before Isis was fast asleep. Lou sighed. Preparations would have to wait, she supposed. She looked down at Isis and smiled.

Chapter 18
A Mystery in the Making

"The distinction between what is real and what is imaginary is not one that can be finely maintained...all existing things are...imaginary."

—John S. Mackenzie (1860–1935), philosopher

The Willow Tree Cottage – 11,000 BCE

What did he mean he found something better? Lunaya attempted to play along. "Oh...? Do tell, my fine-feathered friend. I cannot wait to hear what in the world could be more crucial than locating the Keepers, a Keeper—any Keeper of the age and time I sent you to. Must I remind you of the importance of this task?"

Yuri's feathers were getting a bit ruffled. Of course, he understood the magnitude of his quest. Everyone did. He knew what finding the Keeper of that future time meant. If they could somehow find a Keeper in the time that sat directly across from them on the Wheel of the Ages, perhaps all would not be lost. At least it would allow them to assess how well the teachings had been preserved, and what changes they may need to make as a result.

And if Lunaya would just let him get more than a few words out, perhaps she would understand what he was trying to tell her. He endeavored again to explain: "Was that a rhetorical question? Yes, of course, I understand and am fully aware of the importance of the situation. Which is why I attempted the mission in the first place. I will, of course, return to that time. And I will locate the Keepers. In the meantime, could you please just give me the decency of hearing me out?"

Lunaya sat up in the chair, her curiosity was definitely getting the best of her, along with a healthy dose of the bird's charm. "All right, all right. You have a point. I know you understand. And I am not being fair to you. Go ahead. Tell me what you found."

The raven thought for a long time about how exactly to convey what it was that he did find. He took a long, deep breath. And with that, he began in the best way he knew how—at the beginning.

Chapter 19
A Keeper's Cat

*"Our earliest art, songs, and stories speak
directly of man's relationship with the
nonhuman intelligences alongside which we
inhabit the sentient earth."*

—Brian Froud, *Good Faeries, Bad Faeries*

Maine – 2004

Tuesday afternoon had finally arrived, and along with it its fair share of concerns. There were a few things that had been bothering Lou since her interaction with Jedda the day before. The first one was that, as far as she knew, Jedda had not been a direct descendant of anyone in the Moon Clan. In fact, Lou was sure of it. Her childhood had been spent at "family reunions"— that was what her family had always called these networking events. They were not necessarily get-togethers of close relatives. Instead, they had a different purpose. That purpose was for all the remaining members of the Moon Clan family to unite. It was daunting trying to keep up with everyone sometimes, but being the only Keeper left, it was Lou's responsibility to make sure that the tradition of the Keepers did not end with her.

Usually, the Keepers would show up in a particular family for a few generations, sometimes longer. Not having had any children, though, Lou knew that it was not going to be her direct descendants who would carry on this role. She had made peace with this long ago, which was why she began teaching distant relatives the sacred way. It was tradition for all those of the present day Moon Clan to learn the basic principles, but the deeper truths were usually only shared with those few diligent ones who actually showed interest. Nowadays, there was usually only one Keeper at any given time. Not that there couldn't be more, but most no longer wanted the responsibility; it entailed more than just mastering a few meditation techniques and learning some healing practices along the way. It was about preserving the sacred Faery Wisdom Teachings.

Lou was able to see straight into the hearts and soul records of each individual she worked with. She was convinced she would "see" some sort of indication that they were to become the next Keeper. She never did, though. And most, if not all, of her students eventually became distracted by the burdens of the outside world. Many were not committed to the long journey that was required.

No one even seemed to want to go through the initiations that were required to be a Keeper. The tradition was dying. Lou had started to despair, especially with some of the elders breathing down her neck. Some even dared to question her ability to "see," as if perhaps she had missed something. There were many nasty rumors circling throughout the "family" that Lou had wanted to keep the role, along with all the knowledge and power, for herself, which was absolutely ridiculous. As a Keeper, Lou understood fully well the implications for not passing on the teachings. She had risen way above selfish motives and ego-based actions. It was naturally part of her training as a Keeper. She understood that it was just fear talking with many of them, but there were some with whom it was something far darker.

Standing on the brink of a new age, Lou understood that this opposing energy would only become stronger. It came with the territory. Throughout history, the Turning of the Ages always brought everything to a point of culmination. It didn't make it any easier, though. She also hadn't anticipated that the dissent would rise up from within her family. She had heard legends of that happening in ages past, but she always believed them to be stories. She thought it would be outsiders who would eventually pose a threat to the teachings. She didn't have time to think of the naysayers right now, nor waste her energy on worrying about the Tainted Ones, as those who had lost their way were called.

Lou brushed her thoughts of them far out of mind and returned her attention to Jedda. She really had to think about all of this and the implications that it would entail. Besides, not descending from the Moon Clan was just one thing that was bothering her. The other had to do with something that hit a little closer to home: how in the world had she not recognized Jedda until now? She was stunned, and perhaps even a little self-conscious. She wondered if somehow her abilities had waned a little. Not that she cared at all from a personal standpoint, but the entire future of the Line of Keepers was very possibly riding on this, and she nearly botched it. Jedda had been in her class all school year. It was March! Never once had she even had the slightest inkling that someone outside the Moon Clan could be a possibility, and she certainly hadn't thought or felt it was Jedda. At least not until yesterday. No matter. She needed to get over her wounded pride, and fast. Jedda would be arriving shortly.

Having arrived just moments ago herself, Lou set her things down on the floor hastily. She needed to prepare, but first thing was first: Lou would need to attend to some very important business. "Isis!" Lou called, "Where are you? Mama's home. Come on out, baby girl."

From around the corner, Isis appeared. Her tail bobbed along as her long black and silver form made its way stealthily across the living room to where Lou was standing. "That's a good girl. I missed you. Come here, my sweet." Lou bent down to pick up her overgrown feline friend. Isis gladly allowed herself to be cuddled. She curled up in Lou's arms like a newborn baby and let her head drop back, exposing her neck. This indicated she wanted to be stroked there. Lou could never resist and started to pet her on her neck and belly. Isis started to purr.

Sometimes it helped Lou just to talk aloud, and so she said, "Isis, you know, a new visitor will be arriving shortly. We will need to be very nice and make her feel at home, okay?"

The cat's only response was an increased purring sound. Isis was in seventh heaven.

Lou continued, "This girl who is coming could turn out to be very important to everything we are doing. She could actually be the central piece. I want you to try and be on your best behavior."

If anyone had been standing there with Lou and Isis, they might have decided that Lou was going a little overboard in carrying on these conversations with a cat. That was, of course, because most did not have "ears to hear," for what happened next would have been inaudible to them. Moreover, if they had been able to hear, they might actually have believed they were going a little nutty.

"All right, all right, my Luna. Of course, I will behave. Sheesh! Can't a girl have just a little fun every now and then? From the way you are coaxing me, you'd think I was some confounded beast. A Monster even. Well, I never." Isis finished her tirade.

Lou smiled. She knew Isis wasn't really upset. She just liked to put on a good drama every once in a while. Lou could never get over Isis calling her Luna, though. No one had ever called her by her birth name. Not even her aunt. Isis, however, had refused to call her anything else. The cat insisted that her name was part of her birthright, whatever that meant. Isis said that the birth name, if properly chosen, reflected the soul. She explained it was an energy signature of sorts.

Isis was a Keeper's Cat. Each Keeper had a cat. Always. Some say the tradition went all the way back to the Egyptians; others agreed that it was actually much older. The Keeper's Cats—or Faery Cats, as they were often referred to—had many legends connected to them. The most popular was that the Faery Races, or the Ancient Ones, gave the Keepers the cats long ago, so that they would remember from where their teachings originated. The legend goes on to say that the cats walked right out of the Mists of Faerie and into the arms of the Keepers all at the request of the Faeries. From that point on, they were always guaranteed the loyalty and companionship of a Faery Cat.

To clarify, these were no ordinary cats. Aside from the obvious concerning the story of their origin, these particular cats were very special indeed. They were highly evolved beings that had a profound understanding of reality, so much so that they would often share advice or insight with their Keepers offering a fresh and enlightened perspective. They were also known to chase away trolls, which at one time was a very desirable ability indeed. Troll control wasn't needed as much anymore, but one could never be too careful about such matters.

Additionally, and this was the case with almost all cats in general, they had magnificent capabilities concerning the astral dimensions. Their psychic abilities were unrivaled. Altogether they made for a pretty remarkable ally. It's no wonder that witches were quite fond of them. Lou wasn't a witch, though. She was a Keeper. And that is what she would be attempting to explain to Jedda in just a short while.

Chapter 20
To Grandmother's House We Go

"Look deep into nature and then you will understand everything better."

—Albert Einstein

Maine – 2004

By the time bus 222 arrived at Mayfair Park, Jedda was a wreck. She had been so excited about today that she barely slept the night before. Now her meeting with Miss Silverton was fast approaching, and Jedda found herself ridden with anxiety about what to expect. Perhaps she had romanticized the whole thing. Jedda reminded herself that she was not living in a world of fantasy and magic; this was reality, and in reality, magical things like this did not happen. It was probably just a string of unrelated coincidences that were occurring here. She thought back to her dreams and wondered how many coincidences she could have in such a short period of time.

Jedda alighted from the bus and looked around. There just ahead of her, on the north side of the park, was a house with a red door and shutters—*Miss Silverton's house!* She stared at it awhile before proceeding any further. Jedda recognized she was standing at a major crossroads in her life. Something told her that if she continued, nothing would ever be the same.

She thought about running for a moment. Then she laughed. It was almost as if she didn't have a choice. Of course she did. But she knew that she couldn't walk away. Not anymore. She wouldn't. The what-ifs would kill her. No, there was no turning back now.

Jedda walked up to Miss Silverton's door and rang the bell. She waited. The thought of running occurred to her one last time. Too late, though. The door opened.

"Hi, Jedda. I'm so glad you could make it. We have so much to talk about, you and I. Come inside."

Miss Silverton motioned to the sofa. "You can make yourself comfortable while I fix us a cup of tea and a snack to have during our conversation. What kind of tea do you like, dear?"

"Thanks, Miss Silverton! I'm really looking forward to it." And then Jedda quickly added, "Oh, and anything. Anything but green tea please. Thank you."

Miss Silverton smiled and walked into the kitchen. Jedda plopped down on the couch. A day at school definitely zapped her energy. She again thought about her intense dislike of that place. Then again it had brought her to Miss Silverton. She thought that maybe she needed to start looking for the silver lining.

Miss Silverton called out from the kitchen, "Oh, and Jedda, when we are not at school, please feel free to call me Lou. It's less formal than Miss Silverton, and I never have been much for formalities."

"Uh…okay, Miss Silverton…I mean, Lou. It might take me a bit to get used to, but I will try to remember," Jedda replied just as a large cat came bounding into the living room as if to see what was going on. Jedda noticed the cat immediately. "Oh. Hi, beautiful. And what's your name?"

Lou, overhearing Jedda, peered around the corner, suspiciously eying Isis, and quickly responded, "Why, that's Isis. She must've come out to meet you! She doesn't really like anyone, but she also doesn't like to miss anything either."

Then, directing her next sentence to Isis, she said, "Now you be a good girl and welcome our guest. Be nice."

Jedda couldn't tell if she was teasing. There was a hint of seriousness in Lou's voice. Isis drew closer, and as she did, Jedda exclaimed, "Oh my, you are pretty! What's more is you look just like my cat at home!"

Lou smiled to herself. She called out, "That's nice. You have a cat, dear. What is his or her name?"

"Artemis. His name is Artemis, and…" before Jedda could finish, Lou nearly dropped the tea kettle.

Jedda realized she must have said something disturbing. Not understanding exactly what it was that had flustered her teacher, she began, "Miss Silverton…uh, I mean, Lou, is everything all right?"

Lou composed herself and managed, "Yes, dear, everything is fine..." She didn't even get her half attempt of an excuse out when a voice was heard.

"Well, at least she knows to name properly! Yes, I would concur—everything is fine indeed."

It was hard to tell which of the two were more shocked in that moment. Of course, both Lou and Jedda were both stunned, but for very different reasons. Lou stood frozen like a rigid statue. Jedda stared dumbfounded and wide-eyed like a deer caught in headlights. She was sure she understood now what Alice must have felt upon entering Wonderland. She was speechless, which, for Jedda, was an auspicious event in and of itself. Did she just hear the cat talk? It was impossible. She needed time to stop just long enough to consider the situation at hand, because she was sure that in the next few seconds, her life was going to reach that point of no return, and everything she believed about the nature of reality as she knew it was about to be shattered forever.

The cat continued, "Well, don't everyone stop talking on my account. I mean, I do appreciate being given the floor, but really, I was only making a comment. Actually, I was delivering a compliment. Luna, I do realize that must be hard for you to believe considering I offer them so few and far between. That being said, I was actually being nice. In case you needed me to clarify."

Lou ignored Isis for the time being and walked over to Jedda. "Did you by any chance hear that?" Lou asked. For a second, Lou thought that maybe Jedda hadn't, or rather she was hoping she had not.

Isis answered, not giving Jedda a chance, "Don't be a fool, Luna. Of course, she can hear me. She can clearly hear Artemis, too; otherwise, how else would she have been able to hear his real name and properly name him?"

Jedda finally managed, "You can talk? Or rather, I can hear you talk? How is that possible?"

Upon realizing her mistake, Isis tried to ease the tension in the room by meowing and stretching out on her back as if her cuteness would distract everyone from the situation at hand.

The cat looked at Jedda apologetically. "Sheesh…I'm sorry. I thought you knew. When I look at you, you look as if you can *see*. But you cannot. I realize that now and I'm sorry. I'm not really sure why you appear as if you can see, but you cannot. And I have no idea how you managed to call Artemis by his proper name, but you have."

Then she turned to Lou and, in a genuine voice, added, "Luna, I'm sorry." Isis looked up at Lou and meowed loudly in an attempt to plead her case and regain some favor in her Keeper's eyes. Then Isis gazed back at Jedda, still confused. Suddenly, the Angel of Clarity graced Isis, and something flashed in the cat's eyes that Lou had never seen before: recognition.

Now it was Isis's turn to be stunned. "Luna! Don't you see? Don't you? She carries the energy signature of the Ancient Ones!"

Lou was speechless. How could she not have seen it before? Of course. That would account for everything. Well, sort of. She really had no idea how this was possible, unless there was truth to some of the ancient legends. This was incredible. Had she known, she might have prepared differently, done something differently. There was no use regretting anything now. No, the only direction was forward, and with full steam ahead!

Jedda interrupted Lou's racing thoughts when she raised her voice; she was slightly agitated about all the riddles and ongoing mystery talk that everyone seemed to be using with her lately. She had had it. All the stress of the last couple weeks had reached its boiling point. With that she exploded.

"What is going on here? Someone had better start explaining something to me soon, and I mean it. Not to sound pushy or ungrateful or anything else, Miss Silverton, really. You have to understand where I'm coming from, though. Up until last week I was a normal (well, maybe not normal), but you know what I mean. I was a teenage high school girl with a painfully boring life. Within less than two weeks, I have had strange dreams about a forest and a bird, and some woman or someone. I may have even encountered the same bird outside my house in a willow tree and then talked with him.

"Everyone acts as if they have all the answers, but the more they talk, the more questions that arise! What's worse is that I came over here to gain some clarity on some things, including that darn symbol, and all I have gotten is further down the rabbit hole! Now please forgive me for my growing impatience and my forwardness, but I have reached my limit!"

The floodgate had been opened. There was no stopping it now. For some reason unknown to Jedda, she began to sob. She started crying uncontrollably. She couldn't help it. Each time she tried to continue speaking, a wave of emotion would well up from deep within her and surface as a wretched moan. She must have been holding this back for days now. In all this time, she had shared her recent experiences with no one. It had remained bottled up, and now there was no avoiding the aloneness she felt. Regardless of whether or not it had been done in an appropriate fashion, Jedda had finally released everything that had built up within her. She hadn't realized until now how heavy she had been. She had been walking around with this underlying ache in her whole body. Now it was all being released. She felt exhausted, and she collapsed onto the couch.

Lou sat down on the sofa next to Jedda. She gathered the young girl's crumpled and quivering body into her arms and hugged her for a very long time. That was all it took. Jedda began another round of weeping. Isis, feeling slightly guilty for what she might have had a hand in unleashing, jumped up on the couch and nuzzled her face on Jedda, wanting to ease the girl's troubles. Jedda's weeping started to subside. Nothing had been solved, but for some reason, she started to feel better.

Lou stood up. "All right, honey. We definitely have a lot to talk about. And you are right; you deserve some answers. I will do the best I can. We have a long conversation ahead of us. Let me grab us that tea."

Lou got up and went into the kitchen. Not wanting to give Jedda a chance to become upset again, she quickly chose two chamomile tea bags and popped them each in a teacup. She poured some hot water on top and allowed the tea to steep as she gathered the tiny porcelain teacups and placed them on a tray.

Lou returned to the sofa to find Isis curled up on Jedda's lap. Jedda was scratching her underneath the neck. "Okay, Isis, give Jedda some space. Can't you see she is exhausted?"

"Awww, Luna, come on. Haven't you heard that petting an animal is soothing to the soul?" Isis taunted.

Jedda smiled. She had calmed down considerably by now. She was eagerly waiting to hear what Lou was going to say about all this. Lou set the tray down on the coffee table in front of Jedda. She handed her a cup. Jedda glanced inside, wanting to be sure it didn't contain green tea. Once satisfied, she returned her attention to her host.

Lou began, "I am going to tell you a story. Try to keep an open mind. Also, one more thing—promise me that you will stay to hear the entire story. You must hear me out before you make any decisions. Deal?"

Decisions? Jedda wondered to herself. *What kind of decisions could she possibly have to make that would involve a promise like this?* Jedda waved it away. She was much too interested to finally hear some answers about all of this to worry about any decisions.

She hurriedly held up her right hand and extended her pinky finger and announced: "Deal!" Lou had to chuckle. They pinky swore. Isis jumped up. Apparently, she wanted to be part of the agreement, too. She curled her tail around both their pinkies, and with that Lou began.

Chapter 21
Moon Clan History 101

*"A few groups still achieve these higher
accomplishments. These groups...become a
guiding beacon for the human race as it again
marches on to another high point in
civilization's progress. It is still to be
determined whether the mistakes of a few,
accepted by the majority, can again overwhelm
and carry the great bulk into oblivion for a
great cycle of time."*

—Baird T. Spaulding, *Life and Teaching
of the Masters of the Far East: Volume 3*

Maine – 2004

"According to the history of my people, there is a magical and highly evolved race of beings that has existed for many thousands of years. This race of beings has been known by many names, the most familiar of which being Faery. The Humans and what was known as the Faery race worked closely together, weaving visions of love and light. Eventually, as time passed, only a small group of people continued to live the sacred teachings taught to them by the Faeries. This group became known as the Moon Clan. The Faeries continued to teach the Moon Clan many things, and the Moon Clan swore to uphold sacred law by incorporating the teachings into their daily lives and living them."

Lou continued with the Moon Clan's history. "As time went by, the natural cycle of things took its course. While the importance of maintaining a harmonious relationship with nature was known, it was only a matter of time before everyone would forget who they really were. And, consequently, their connection with the Earth would seemingly be lost. Long ago, these cycles of the Earth were understood by humans.

"Back then it was understood that time was not linear, but more circular. Most importantly, there is a dark downward spiral of each cycle, as well as a corresponding upward spiral of light. During the dark period of a cycle, the energy of the Earth becomes very heavy and dense. Difficult it is for the light particles to come through. This manifests outwardly in all kinds of upheaval and disharmony, such as violence, manipulation, and war. Fear is felt because people begin to see themselves as separate."

Isis had been purring up until that point. Then a tiny meow was let out. Lou acknowledged, "Oh yes. Okay, Isis, you tell the next part. Isis loves to talk about the Age of Awakening."

Isis did not move from her spot on Jedda's lap but gladly took over.

"Thank you, Luna. You know I do love to focus on the Light. So where were we? Ah yes. So, of course, following the natural order, the cycle eventually makes its swing upward, and the Age of Light brings with it light frequencies that awaken our consciousness. The energy of the planet is lifted during this period, and humans move back into harmonious relationship with all of life everywhere."

Isis appeared to be satisfied with her explanation of the Age of Light, and so she let Lou continue.

"These cycles always carry great lessons with them. When the lessons are not paid attention to, however, they tend to repeat themselves. The hope is to eventually master these lessons; this would allow all to move forward on their evolutionary path upon the Earth Mother. You see, it is all really a dance in consciousness. It is really the journey of consciousness on Earth evolving."

Jedda was able to follow along quite easily. This was not unlike some of the information that she enjoyed reading about in all her books. She was very thoughtful about all that she was hearing.

"So, you are saying that the cycles weren't necessarily good or bad, although they might have appeared that way. They were just different energies like seemingly asleep or enlightened?"

"They *are*," Lou corrected emphatically and continued. "The cycles were not a thing of the past. As long as we are in physical form, the cycles continue to be a part of our daily experience. Earth still goes through these cycles. Nothing has changed, other than man's ability to recognize and understand these great patterns."

Jedda caught on quickly. "Wow. So wait a minute. If these cycles are still going on but no one knows about it, then that sounds like we have forgotten. You said people forget about the rhythm of nature in the dark part of the cycle, or the Age of Sleep...so are you saying that we are in an Age of Sleep?" Jedda was fascinated.

Although she had demonstrated astute capabilities in class, Lou was pleased that Jedda was promising to be such a quick study regarding this sublime material. She confirmed Jedda's supposition.

"Yes, Jedda, that's right. We have been in an Age of Sleep for a very long time now, about 13,000 years. And now, right now, we are standing once again on the brink of time. We are on the precipice, and we can almost see the Age of Awakening that is before us. There are a lot of theories on when exactly that shift will occur, but the point is we are finally at the end of the Sleeping Cycle."

Jedda was amazed and excited. Lou could tell this by her glowing expression. Her face came alive, often the result of hearing deep truth and resonating deeply with it. A light could be seen reflected in her eyes.

"Anyway, about 13,000 years ago the Earth was approaching this Sleep Cycle, and as preparation for this Age of Darkness, the Moon Clan wished to see to it that the Faery Wisdom Teachings were preserved. A Great Gathering was called, and…"

Jedda was confused, "A Great Gathering?"

Isis chimed in. "Yes, a Great Gathering was a meeting between the Faery Races and the elders of the Moon Clan. It would convene to discuss serious issues and changing energies upon the Earth."

Lou smiled and continued, "So, at this particular Great Gathering, it was determined that from within the Moon Clan would originate a successive line of individuals or group of individuals that would be tasked to carry on the teachings at all costs. In this way, the sacred way would survive. This thread of living light became known as the Order of the Keepers."

Chapter 22
The Tradition of the Keepers

"As we humans moved away from our close connection with the earth, we lost our link with the wild folk. We forgot how to see them, how to contact them, and how to treat them."

—Anna Franklin, *Working with Faeries*

Maine – 2004

L ou continued. "The Faeries taught the Keepers a great deal about the trees in particular. They showed them how the trees stored within their rings the Wisdom of the Ages, and if one could learn Elyrie, the Language of the Trees, one could understand all this and more. The Language of the Trees was a language of symbols and images that spoke to your heart and soul. As such, it was like a living stream of wisdom that was more of a practice. This study came to be known as the Tree Mysteries."

Jedda mused to herself aloud, "Trees, huh? I always knew I felt something special when I was among them. They have always drawn me…"

Lou smiled as if Jedda's comment had confirmed something for her. She continued somewhat begrudgingly. "Unfortunately, and just as predicted, the Moon Clan, eventually succumbing to the chaos and darkness of the Sleeping Cycle of the Earth, slowly began to degenerate. This left only a small remnant behind."

Jedda was astounded that such a seemingly advanced and cohesive people could dwindle in this way. She asked about this. "So there are only a few of the Moon Clan left today?"

Now Lou's smile was betrayed by the underlying sadness in her voice. "Not exactly. There are numerous descendants of the Moon Clan. However, there is only a handful remaining of those of us who still know, understand, and practice the sacred way based on the Faery Wisdom Teachings."

Lou was feeling the weight of her burden very prominently upon her shoulders now. She breathed as if to steady herself for the final blow that almost never passed from her lips, for it was such a grueling acknowledgement that it had been almost impossible for her ancestors to come to terms with it. The utter shame that they must have experienced when they first realized what was happening was incomprehensible. Tears began streaming from Lou's eyes.

Jedda could see that her teacher was personally affected by whatever it was she wanted to reveal. She also had a feeling that this was more than a mythological story, and somehow her teacher felt deeply connected to it. She wanted to be helpful and supportive. She thought about what silver lining she might add to this heavy-laden cloud.

"Lou, what is it? What's wrong? I mean, I know that the Moon Clan has mostly forgotten, but I'm sure they tried their hardest. And, and, well…I'm sure they could always learn again. About the sacred teachings I mean. It's never too late, right?"

Lou brightened a little, if only for the genuine attempt that her student was making to cheer her up. "No, Jedda, you are right. I suppose it's never too late." She thought carefully about how she wanted to say the thing she couldn't bear to admit. This was a wound that ran deep, and it carried with it a sense of misplaced identity. Lou swallowed hard.

Isis knew and understood the struggle that Lou was undergoing. Without delay, being the supportive and sympathetic cat that she was, Isis took over from there.

"Earth moved deeper and deeper into the Age of Sleep. And as the Moon Clan succumbed more and more to the dark energies, the unthinkable happened: the Keepers lost their ability to access the records in the tree rings, and consequently they have largely forgotten the Language of the Trees."

As Isis uttered that final sentence, Lou burst in a tidal wave of pain and wretchedness. Her sobs were loud and thunderous. It was as if an ocean of collective guilt and suffering of Lou and all her ancestors had been trapped inside of her. Unconsciously, each Keeper since that very sad day had felt an immense obligation to somehow restore what had been lost and reclaim this key part of their ancient wisdom as it was known and practiced so long ago. Lou was no exception. For the first time, Lou gave herself permission to fully feel all of this. As she did, the tears began to lessen, leaving behind only minor aftershocks. These caused her body to quiver gently like ripples on the surface of a pond after a pebble had been cast.

Then she was empty. She was empty, and she was glad for it. Surprisingly, she felt a little lighter. Simply sharing this story had been profoundly healing. Lou started once again. Her voice sounded more confident and poised.

"This brings us to the present," Lou said finally. She hadn't realized how difficult it was going to be to sum that history up like that. What a labor!

Jedda appeared surprised, "That's it. *That* brings us to the present? How did it go? What about all the Keepers? What happened to them after they forgot?"

Lou waited patiently for her to finish then added, "Of course, that is not it. But the rest is not important for now. You see, Jedda, I am a Keeper," Lou paused for impact.

Jedda was silent. She definitely hadn't expected that. Up until now, it just sounded like a good story. She had had an inkling that Lou was connected in some way, especially upon seeing how upset she had become. She figured it had more to do with an old wives' tale that had been passed down through her family or something. She assumed it to be more conceptual, perhaps a folktale meant to teach a moral. She didn't realize it was true. Not really.

Lou's revelation had not even had time to sink in before she concluded, "And what's more is that I believe that somehow, and I'm not quite sure how just yet...but I do believe that...well...you are, too!"

Chapter 23
A Raven's Tale

*"We do not yet live fully in the fourth
dimension, and once this dimension is fully
integrated we will see that all time—past,
present, and future—exists simultaneously on
the spiral ladder of evolution."*

—Thea Summer Deer, *Wisdom
of the Plant Devas*

Willow Tree Cottage – 11,000 BCE

Yuri began his tale from the beginning. As he
started to talk, though, Lunaya gazed off into
space. She had been so excited to hear his tale, but
something Yuri said about "the beginning" triggered
something within her. She thought back to where it had
all started for her. She wasn't even sure anymore. She
began reviewing her life in her mind. She was
remembering back years ago when she still lived in the
community with her people.

Yuri must have realized he lost her somewhere along the way. "Lunaya, have you heard anything that I have said? Anything at all?"

Lunaya felt sad. "I'm sorry, Yuri. I was just thinking about everything, and wondering…well…was it worth it?"

The tradition of Keepers had been started generations ago within the Moon Clan as the agreed upon outcome that had emerged from the last Great Gathering. The Faeries had agreed to teach a group of individuals the deepest and most sacred teachings of their tradition—the Tree Mysteries.

This great honor had been a custom in Lunaya's family—her mother and her mother's mother before that. She had come from a long line of Keepers. Like it had been for all those before her, the role of Keeper was felt to be a great privilege, but also with it came its fair share of responsibility. Sometimes the responsibility felt so great it carried the weight of a thousand burdens. Other times, Lunaya could not help but marvel at all the miracles her life had been filled with as a result of it.

In any case, Lunaya would not run from her destiny, not that she could really escape it even if she had wanted to, for it was etched on her soul from the moment she was born. At least that was what she told herself. This was why she had chosen to do the only thing she knew to do to guarantee that the teachings survived—she would move deep into the Forest and live among the Faeries; this would ensure that the human and Faery relations remained strong. It would also help to maintain a connection with nature, for as the dark part of the cycle was approaching, this was becoming more and more difficult.

Lunaya could not fathom forgetting her connection to nature, nor the idea of losing the ability to hear the trees. Unfortunately, her plan had not come without a great price—for in order to carry it out, she had to leave her friends, family, and community—everyone whom she loved dearly, including her cherished twin brother. She would not have done it if she had not believed it to be completely necessary. Not that it was a requirement of a Keeper to be alone. The stakes were higher now, however, and the risks were much greater.

Yuri felt sympathetic toward Lunaya. He knew how much she had sacrificed to carry out her purpose. He wished sometimes he could help her bear the burden, but he was only a bird. That was why he had decided to help her in the only way in which he was able.

"Lunaya, listen to me. I cannot pretend to understand what you are feeling. I am a bird, and do not have these same experiences. You have been such a strong force in this whole process. You have kept your promise to the best of your ability, and some would argue that you have gone far beyond what anyone had ever expected of you. Your will has been unbending. Your dedication and commitment to this cause has been incessant. And so, it is my turn to remind you of your purpose, and why we set out to do what we did in the first place."

There had been so much uncertainty surrounding this Turning of the Ages. The ethers were cloudy, and many—including Lunaya—were having extreme difficulty knowing what steps to take. No one yet knew for sure in what great outward event the Turn of the Ages might manifest, for it was always different: a pole shift, an ice age, a flood. It was anyone's guess; however, there was, according to the Faery Ones, an event on the horizon that could be the determining factor in the outcome.

Yuri's encouragement made her perk up. Even if only for a moment, it was enough to get her going. "Right. I thought that if I could somehow establish a connection with a future point in time, then maybe I could gain some insight as to what further preparations still needed to be made…"

Yuri was grateful that his bit of encouragement had seemed to work. "Yes, exactly. So you even went to Elysinia to consult with her about her opinion on the subject. Even she confirmed that, theoretically, it could work."

Lunaya had thought back to that meeting. She had met with the Faery Elder to discuss the feasibility of the idea. Elysinia had concurred that meeting with a Keeper of a future age might give them a greater indication as to what to expect. She wasn't sure, however, if Elysinia had been referring to the coming Age of Darkness, or something else. The Faery elder had nonchalantly mentioned the possibility of a very auspicious event occurring in the near future. The way she spoke about it, Lunaya surmised that she could only be referring to one thing.

The Crossing of the Frog and the Mushroom? Lunaya couldn't believe it. That she had not received word from Maob or the other Moon Clan elders that the magical conjunction would soon occur further confirmed her rising suspicions.

"Remind me why we wanted to do this. I mean, so what? So we establish a connection with a Keeper at some point in a future timeline. Oh, Yuri, forgive me. I am having a moment of self-pity."

Lunaya sat with her hand pressed against her forehead. She was being a little dramatic. Yuri struggled to maintain his cool about him.

"Not any future point, Lunaya. The one that stands directly across from ours. Remember, you said it yourself, 'One cannot prepare for the present without giving equal respect to and honoring the space/time that sits opposite it on the Wheel of the Ages. For it is in the complement that all of life can find a balance.' Remember? Oh, for goodness' sake, Lunaya, snap out of it. I didn't fly 13,000 years into the future for you to lose your wits about you!"

Yuri had been sought out for just this purpose. For Yuri, timeline walking was something that, with a little effort, could definitely be managed. They had decided he would locate a Keeper at the beginning of the next Age of Light. Elysinia had been unusually intrigued to know what this mission might turn up.

All Yuri had to do was follow the golden thread of the Order of the Keepers. This should have led him straight to a Keeper of that future age. If he succeeded in piercing the veil of time, the rest would be a piece of cake. Or so Lunaya had thought.

She quickly got a hold of herself. Within seconds, Lunaya was back on track. She waited for Yuri to begin the retelling of his tale. This time he had her complete attention. She knew he was a master at traveling between the worlds, so what could have gone wrong?

Yuri gladly picked up where he had left off. "So everything went according to plan. I launched and found myself flying through what felt like a whirlpool. I continued to follow the golden thread of Keepers though the ages, just as you had instructed me. Sometimes I noticed the thread grow thin and weak; at other times, it strengthened. It never did stop, however. I followed it. I didn't just see it; I sensed its corresponding vibration, too, which gently pulled me forward. I flew and flew for what seemed like hours, days, even weeks. All was going well until I lost the thread."

Lunaya looked at him astounded. "You did what? How could you lose the thread?"

Yuri didn't know how he had lost it. He had been trekking along just fine. He had no idea where he had made a wrong turn, if indeed he even had made a wrong turn.

He continued, "Well, I'm not sure exactly. But that's when I found myself being drawn into the dream plane. Interestingly, that was where I began to pick up the signal of the Keepers again. This is where it gets weird, though."

This is where it gets weird, thought Lunaya. *Oh, boy.* She didn't interrupt, though.

"Although I could sense the signal, I definitely could not see the thread any longer. I didn't know what else to do, so I decided to follow the signal to see where it would take me."

Lunaya was completely engrossed. She had not foreseen Yuri losing the signal. Of course she knew there was a chance that the Line of Keepers wouldn't have survived the Age of Sleep, in which case the signal would have gone dead. She shuddered to think about such a tragic possibility. She waited for Yuri to go on with his fascinating tale.

"I wandered through the dream plane on a hunch when, suddenly, I realized I was no longer in neutral territory. I don't know when it happened exactly, but at some point, I crossed over into someone's dreamtime space. Unexpectedly, I found myself back in the Forest. I saw the Great Oak up ahead, so I flew toward it and landed on one of its higher branches to get my bearings. One of the Ancient Ones, Elysinia, was below me, accessing the records from the rings of the tree. That's when I saw her. I saw this young girl in the Forest. She did not belong there, and yet somehow she did. She was a part of the Forest somehow, yet she had been observing the scene as if it were completely foreign to her senses. That's when I realized it. She had the energy of a Keeper!"

"Wait a minute. You said you didn't find a Keeper. Now you are telling me that you did indeed find a Keeper?" Lunaya interrupted Yuri's story. She was completely confused and a little irritated. Why did working with this bird always have to result in riddles?

He either found a Keeper or he didn't. And in this case, it sounded like he had.

She got up and started to pace. "Bird, you better start explaining yourself. I have grown to like you, but that could change very quickly. Why are you playing games?"

Yuri sighed, trying to make up for the patience that Lunaya seemed to lack. "Lunaya, if you would let me finish, you might understand what I am trying to tell you. She doesn't know she is a Keeper."

"What? That's impossible. How could one not know she were a Keeper? I don't understand. You mean she is part of the Moon Clan but hasn't been initiated as a Keeper yet. Okay, so why didn't you keep moving and go to a current Keeper of the time?" Apparently, Lunaya seemed to think this was so cut and dry.

Exhausted, Yuri struggled to continue again. "After making this discovery, I decided to make contact with her. I tell you, not only does she have no conscious awareness of being a Keeper, I can assure you she knows nothing about the Moon Clan. But above that, there's more…"

Yuri paused for impact. Lunaya was still processing the last bit that he had revealed. Lunaya looked up at him. He definitely had her attention now.

He went on, "When I was in her dream, I was watching her. Then she saw me. She could see me! But more incredibly, she could see Elysinia accessing the records. I read it in her face. She could see. Do you understand what I'm telling you?"

Lunaya understood all right. At least she thought she did up until this moment. Now she didn't feel entirely certain about anything. She was deep in thought. "How could it be possible? Other than the Keepers trained within the Moon Clan, the only ones able to naturally access and read the ancient records stored in the rings of the trees are..." her thoughts trailed off as Yuri began hopping around excitedly.

He knew the magnitude of what he had just revealed; they both did. He was waving his wings uncontrollably now and flailing about. He couldn't contain himself any longer. And he couldn't wait for Lunaya to draw the obvious conclusion here. Losing all self-control, the raven blurted out, "Lunaya! She is of the Faery Race!"

Chapter 24
A Dream Worth Keeping

"In the morning of life came the good fairy with
her basket and said, 'Here are gifts. Take one,
leave the others. And be wary, choose wisely;
oh, choose wisely! for only one of them is
valuable.' The gifts were five: fame, love,
riches, pleasure, death."

—Mark Twain, *The Five Boons of Life*

Moon Clan community – 11,000 BCE

Master Ra-Ma'at awoke from another dream about his beloved. He had dreamt often of her face, her tenderness, her gentle touch, and her beauty. Just being in her presence was like being kissed by moonlight. Her skin gave off a radiance comparable to the North Star. She was of the Faery Race. The Moon Clan people had a long history of working alongside the Faery Races since before anyone could remember. This was probably what earned them their name as clan of the

Moon, for their way was so intertwined with the rhythms of nature that they were likened to it.

Unfortunately, this deep-seated connection with the Earth and all her magical creatures was coming to a close, at least for the majority. The Age of Sleep was nearly upon them now, and so the darkness would continue to settle in. Sleep was starting to gain a foothold in the hearts of men, and so over the last century, Faery and Human relations had become strained. The veil between the worlds was coming to a close. This was inconceivable to the Moon Clan, for they could not envision a life separate from nature, nor void of magic. Master Ra-Ma'at could not imagine a life separate from his beloved.

Master Ra-Ma'at allowed a tear to trickle down his cheek. Wanting to be strong and support her choice, he had remained silent. How many times had his mind played over and over the events of those last few days he had spent with her! If he had to do it again, he would not have acted so indifferently. He imagined himself talking her out of it somehow or at the very least voicing his opinion. She was the love of his life, and he did not want her to leave. He understood that her people needed her, but he couldn't bear life without her. For, surely, whatever she was able to accomplish on her own, they could accomplish even greater by working together.

"We will always be together," she had told him. She had taken his hand and placed it on her heart. "This is where our love and connection will live forever." Then she had walked away into the Mists of the Forest to return to her people.

Oftentimes, he would dream of that day. In his dream, he would do what he hadn't dared and call out after her. "Elysinia! Don't go!"

It was a dream such as this that woke him from his tormented sleep. He sat up in bed. Embarrassed that someone might have heard him, Master Ra-Ma'at finished his thought in a suppressed whisper. "Stay with me please…"

As he struggled to gain his bearings, he noticed a flutter in the space within his heart. At long last, a Great Gathering! He could feel the invitation resting gently upon his heart and soul. The time had come, and he was glad for it. He knew he had to go to the Great Gathering place. He knew he would see Elysinia there. Then he could tell her about the darkness that he could feel advancing. He wanted to discuss the prophecy held within the Crystal Library, and how it might have something to do with all of this.

Then and only then would he also take the time to share all the hurt and pain he had felt as a result of losing her. Most importantly, he would tell Elysinia the one thing he had wished he would have said on that sad day of departure so long ago: "We will find another way. We must!"

Chapter 25
A Disciple's Heart

"The face of truth is hidden by thy golden orb,
O Sun. That do thou remove, in order that I,
Who am devoted to truth, may behold its glory."

—Isha Upanishad, XV

Moon Clan Community – 11,000 BCE

The decision was final. Master Ra-Ma'at would venture deep into the Forest to attend the Great Gathering. There was one thing he knew for certain. After the Great Gathering, he did not intend to return—not without Elysinia. If she declined, he would remain with her in her realm. Originally, she had refused to entertain any idea of him coming along with her. She was adamant about the impact of his work with the young initiates in training. He had his destiny, and she had hers. Well, his work was coming to a close now. Taivyn would be the last pupil he would take on, and that had only been at the request of the Council of Five.

Delivered by a Faery Emissary, the written request had been in the form of a letter forged in moonlight.

He brushed that whole situation from his mind. He didn't have time to think about all the mysterious circumstances surrounding Taivyn's appearance. It was time to go. He summoned his most trusted companion and scribe, Korin. He would have Korin see to it that his disappearance was thoroughly explained at the appropriate time. He couldn't have anyone trying to dissuade him from going on this journey alone.

A short, stocky young man with dark eyes arrived promptly at sundown at the Master's door. Master Ra-Ma'at let him in. He stole a peek down the long corridor to make sure no one was around and hurried Korin inside. He did so very quickly, and so he did not notice Taivyn bumbling down the hall from the other direction. The door closed behind them, but none too soon, for Taivyn was sure he had seen Korin being pulled inside by the Master. What in the world was going on? It was highly unlike Master Ra-Ma'at to meet secretly even with other Keepers, for the master was a Sun Keeper, and nothing he ever did was secret or kept "in the dark." He said that this was a principle he learned from the sun: to shine forth the light of truth and to illuminate the path for all to see.

So one can imagine just how strange it must have appeared to young Taivyn when he saw Master Ra-Ma'at in this covert meeting with one of the younger Keepers. Taivyn had noticed the Master acting strangely as of late, but this certainly took the cake. It must have been this extremely bizarre incident that caused Taivyn to resort to what he did next. Taivyn Green waited in the shadows of the corridor to see what these two were up to.

Master Ra-Ma'at reluctantly began his explanation to Korin. "Korin, first, I want to thank you for answering my call and coming so swiftly."

Korin started to say something when Master Ra-Ma'at held up his hand. "Please let me finish. A Great Gathering has been called, and I have decided to attend it. I will be gone for a while, as there are certain circumstances that need attending to. I am entrusting you with a great deal. I want you to continue the education of the young ones on the Path. And I want you to pay particular attention to Taivyn. He is at a ripe age and very soon will demonstrate whether or not he is cut out for the *Path of the Keeper*."

Korin could not believe what he was hearing. He was flabbergasted. "Master, I don't understand what you are saying! What do you mean you are leaving? Why do you make it sound as if you do not intend to return? You are coming back, aren't you?"

Master Ra-Ma'at knew it was not going to be easy for Korin or any of the others for that matter. "Listen to me, Korin. I know this is difficult, but I need you to be strong. That courageous heart that you have cultivated so well...that is what you are going to need right now. As for where I am going, all I can say is that I am going into the Forest. I will go first to join the Lady Lunaya, my sister and elder Keeper of the Moon Clan. Then together we will go to convene with the Council of Five of the Faery Races."

Korin was shocked. He barely remembered the Lady Lunaya. She had left when he was just a boy. He wondered if she would be returning to the community soon? Was that why the Master was going to meet her?

Master Ra-Ma'at was not ready to offer a full disclosure. "Korin, this is something that must be done, and as one of the elders, I must do it. That is enough for now. When the time is right, I would like you to inform the others that I have departed. Make no remark as to when I might return, for in truth, I do not know that myself. I have sent word to the other elders of my intentions to attend the Great Gathering. I would assume I should see most of them there. In the case that I do not return, you will know what to do, as you will be the one to take my place. This explains what I have just told you and carries my seal, so the community will have no doubts as to my intentions and wishes in my absence." Master Ra-Ma'at handed Korin a small scroll.

A dollop of sarcasm came over Korin unexpectedly. "Right, because it is quite unbelievable that you would just simply abandon the Moon Clan, all your work, everything…"

Korin's voice became faint then, and he could feel himself on the verge of crying. He hadn't meant to sound so disrespectful. He didn't know what had come over him. The Master was like a father to him. The thought of him leaving was just too much to bear, and he started to feel the familiar sense of abandonment rising up to rear its ugly head. It was a classic example of déjà vu.

The beginning years of Korin's spiritual work had been solely focused on healing the wound from his past. It was a great emotional wound that resulted from his father leaving his mother and him behind. The abandonment had been so traumatic for Korin that an emotional block developed in his energy field. As impossible as it had seemed at the beginning, Master Ra-Ma'at had insisted that he work to heal this before he began any further spiritual training. The Master had explained that one could not proceed in this work if they themselves were not clear of any emotional baggage.

He recalled the Master's first words to him on the subject: "Korin, if you endeavor to be a healer, you must first heal yourself. You cannot see clearly when you have an emotional wound. It colors everything you do. When a block exists, all external situations are viewed or perceived through the filter of this block or faulty thought. Your desire to be a healer stems from your inner desire to be healed. When you are ready to begin your healing process, you may return to me. I will act as a guide through your entire healing journey."

He had finally returned to the Master. And when he did, Korin dove head first into the healing work. He was ready. He wanted to be whole. That was many years ago. Since then, Korin had not only cleared the wound but had also gone on to study further with the Master. He went through all the initiations required of the Keepers.

Of course, after moving through his healing journey, he had no desire to be a healer. The Master had been right. His earlier desire had been the projection of what he himself had needed. Toward the end of his training, Korin had begun to gravitate toward teaching. So upon completion of the program, that was exactly what he did. He started teaching the young ones who desired to pursue the Path of the Keeper. He loved it.

Every now and then, there was a heckler who would emerge among the bunch that disturbed the others, but that was all part of it. Taivyn was his current misfit, but he knew that the boy had come a long way. After all, he too, had been seemingly abandoned, although no one really knew for sure what the story surrounding his origin was. For this reason, Korin was sometimes a little tougher on him than the other students. Korin knew that one had to be pushed to succeed. He wasn't going to coddle Taivyn just because of his past. It was no excuse, as Korin had proven. One could still soar to great heights regardless of their predisposition.

It was all this that caused Korin to wonder if he had healed completely. After all this time, all this personal work, how he still managed to attract this sort of experience was impossible for him to understand at this moment. Korin fought hard to hold back the tears.

Not void of humanity, the Master felt a great deal of compassion for his beloved protégé. He knew this would be difficult on everyone, but he understood that it would be especially challenging for Korin. To Korin, the Great Gathering was some abstract event that had taken place in the past. The gathering had not been convened in decades, and definitely not in Korin's lifetime. The Master encouraged him in a soothing voice filled with kindness.

"Korin, my dearest pupil. This is to be a great test of strength for you, and I realize that. I am not abandoning you. There are things that I cannot explain to you now, not because I do not want to and not because I do not trust you, but because I simply do not have time. Time is of the essence. Although many will believe that I go for personal reasons—and that is not completely inaccurate—there are other reasons, far bigger than you and I. There are forces that are outside of our control, and they are greater than either of us are able to fathom at this time, for they are surely unparalleled in our human history as we know it."

Korin tried to make sense of what the Master was saying. He knew he had to check his ego at the front door, so to speak, if he was to carry out this task that the Master was asking of him. He would do a little self-inquiry later to see if there was any emotional residue of that seemingly forgotten wound that still needed to be cleared. He winced at the thought of it. After all this time, could there still be another layer of healing that had to occur? He didn't want to think about it now. In the present moment, Korin had to pull it together and move forward. He would not fail the Master. He could not let him down. Something the Master said was nagging at him, though.

"Master Ra-Ma'at, when you speak of the reasons to carry out this quest, are you referring to the cycles and the coming Age of Sleep? We have been preparing for this for decades, centuries even. Isn't that why Lady

Lunaya went into the Forest in the first place? I don't understand what has changed…"

The Master Ra-Ma'at couldn't help but sigh. Korin was partly right. What Korin was not aware of was the dreams and visions that the Master had been having since the last new moon. His dreams told of something else lurking ahead, something much darker and quite sinister.

The Master was pensive, as he was pondering how much he wanted to divulge. He thought about it briefly and finally determined that in this case, less was more.

"Korin, all I can tell you is that our preparations are not yet over, nor are they sufficient from what I am seeing. Something unforetold has developed on the horizon, and I must do what I can to ensure that all our efforts have not been in vain."

Reluctantly, Korin conceded, for in actuality, he did not really have a choice in this case. Master Ra-Ma'at had spoken, and Korin had already crossed the line with his selfish objections. Luckily, the Master was very forgiving. He knew Korin's heart, and he knew Korin's intentions were well-meaning. Korin nodded his understanding and turned to go. Then he remembered one other thing the Master had said that had piqued his curiosity.

"Oh, Master, just out of curiosity…surely, there are other students currently who are at the same age as Taivyn, who will soon need to choose whether they wish to continue down the Path of the Keeper or not. If it isn't out of place to ask, why did you call my attention to him?"

The Master cursed under his breath. Korin was too smart for his own good. Why did he have to question everything? The Master decided to throw him a proverbial bone and answered, "Korin, again, your questions could take me the day to answer, and I do not have all the time in the world, you see. But I will tell you this: the mysterious circumstances surrounding his appearance, and possibly his birth—although I have not had the time to verify this—might correlate to an ancient prophecy concerning these times. If this turns out to be true, well, then it is imperative that we not only keep an eye on him but that we do everything in our power to see that he develops spiritually. Of course, there is free will, and nothing can be forced upon another, so he does eventually have to choose. That being said, we can do all we can to support the process and hope for the best. Again, nothing of what I have just told you has been confirmed, including the part about whether or not he is indeed the one of which the prophecy foretells. It is just my gut."

The Master didn't give Korin a chance to ask anything further. He hurried Korin toward the door, explaining he was very busy and had much to do before he began his journey into the Forest. His aim was to leave by nightfall, which is why he did not have time to meet and discuss with the entire community. Korin would act as his spokesperson in that regard.

Taivyn, who had been listening the whole time, quickly scurried around the nearby corner and ducked into a small passageway. He pressed his back up against the wall, praying that he would not be discovered. What he had just done was completely unacceptable and against every principle that the Moon Clan taught and stood for. He did not do it with any malicious intent; he simply couldn't help himself when it came to his inquisitiveness, which often turned into nosiness.

Taivyn heard Korin exit Master Ra-Ma'at's study. Korin was completely caught off guard with that last bit of information that the Master had revealed. Of course, the Master had emphasized that nothing was confirmed, but Korin had worked alongside the Master long enough to know that the Master's "gut feelings" usually proved accurate.

As Korin traveled down the hall, his footsteps became less and less pronounced, indicating that he had gone off in the other direction. Eventually, Taivyn could not hear them any longer. He breathed a sigh of relief and relaxed. He slunk down the wall, dropping his bottom to the cold stone floor. He did not know what to make of the conversation he had just overheard. It caused so many questions to arise within him. He did not know which parts were more fascinating: the cycles of time, the unfinished preparations, the talk of the Great Gathering, the Faeries whom he had never seen and was not even certain still existed, or that he might be part of some ancient prophecy. Could they really have been talking about him? What was going on here?

Well, one thing was for certain: he was not about to get any information out of Korin, who still viewed him as an insolent little twerp. Besides, Korin seemed to be in the dark concerning a lot of what was taking place here anyway. By his questions, he had sounded shocked and confused—maybe even a little hurt. No, he definitely was not going to bother Korin for any answers. Taivyn had to know what the Master was planning, though. He could not handle not pursuing it, as he was overflowing with curiosity. Besides, Taivyn surely had a right to know if he was part of some ancient prophecy. Perhaps he could even help. That left one solution—he would have to follow Master Ra-Ma'at into the Forest.

Chapter 26
Into the Forest

"In a sense, therefore, we are actually breathing in the stars—breathing in their essence, so that all these now have a share in our own being. That they must do so is quite a thought, since it suggests that the firmament might be much closer to ourselves than we think, and certainly cannot be apart from us.

—White Eagle, *Spiritual Unfoldment Two*

Moon Clan Community – 11,000 BCE

Master Ra-Ma'at knew that the final tidbit about the prophecy concerning Taivyn would keep Korin busy for days, as there was no shortage of ancient prophecies among the Moon Clan people. The search would be futile, however, because the record containing that prophecy was stored within a crystal, and that crystal could only be found within the Crystal Library in the Realm of Faerie. Who knew if the prophecy was referring to Taivyn, but one couldn't be too careful. Now he just needed to make ready for departure.

Master Ra-Ma'at gathered up all the things he absolutely needed: a few herbs, a scroll with a map of the Forest and its corresponding ley lines, and some rations of brown bread, cheese, fruit, and a flask of fresh water. He placed it all in the center of a square cloth. He gathered up the ends and tied them together with a rope, forming a travel bundle.

Darkness finally set in, revealing the sparkling lights of stars and unidentified flying objects that sporadically frequented the night sky. Master Ra-Ma'at waited patiently until the sounds and voices of those still awake finally died down. He grabbed his staff and without further delay, he embarked on his journey.

He crept beyond the community walls. Noises of the mundane world faded away and a certain stillness set in, allowing the sounds of the night to take the main stage. Crickets, night birds, and a frog could be heard as they played a nocturnal symphony that welcomed the dusk. Master Ra-Ma'at listened closely and smiled. He was almost certain he had heard the frog's uniquely intoxicating serenade, only sung in preparation for a very special and auspicious occasion. He had not received word from any of the elders that the Crossing of the Frog and the Mushroom was occurring any time soon. After all, it was Maob who had been tasked to chart the Mushroom's movements. Surely, he would have sent word to indicate that the time of crossing was approaching. He had hoped he had not missed something like this. He waved the thought away. He could not give in to such mental indulgences now. He would need all his acumen to attend to the quest ahead.

He heard the frog's melody sound again. *Impossible,* he thought to himself. Then again, when one had lived as long as he had, one came to realize that nothing was impossible—implausible maybe, but never impossible. Perhaps this might account for some of his unanswered questions, and perhaps even his disconcerting dreams. If he was truly hearing what he thought he was hearing, then his quest was timely indeed. He would need to make haste.

Master Ra-Ma'at arrived at the Forest's border. He lingered a moment before entering. This was it. He was about to venture deeper into the Forest than he had been in years. Once he embarked, there was no turning back. He checked his inner guidance one last time to make sure this was the correct course of action to take. He got a strong response in the affirmative. This was it. To the Great Gathering and beyond. Without further procrastination, Master Ra-Ma'at slipped into the Forest unseen, or so he thought.

Master Ra-Ma'at took out the scroll he had brought with him and unrolled it. He examined the map before him, paying close attention to the ley lines of the area. He gazed up into the night sky, noting the positions of the stars and their constellations in order to help determine his location.

There was a lot more to the Master's plan than he had revealed to Korin. Unfortunately, it had been necessary to be vague, for Korin did not need to worry his mind with all the details; his focus needed to be on the community, particularly the young ones. Nevertheless, the Master felt a little sad that he was not completely forthcoming with his protégé. He quickly brought his attention back to his devised plan.

After finding Lunaya, he and his sister would make their way toward the place of the Great Gathering; he could feel the invitation gently resting within his heart. The time for this great meeting of minds, hearts, and souls was upon them once again. The Great Gathering would consist of the Faery Council of Five, the elders of the Moon Clan, any interested members of the animal kingdom, and perhaps one from the Celestial Brotherhood.

The Council of Five represented the Five Faery Clans known to reside on the Earth. Many of them had originated from the stars. These Faery Clans had been known to the Moon Clan for aeons of time. Master Ra-Ma'at did not know exactly how long their kinds had been working together side by side. For many years, Ra-Ma'at himself had counseled with them. They were trusted allies, Guardians of the Earth, and the true Keepers of the Trees, for they had within them the natural ability to access, read, and understand the Records of Time stored within the trees' rings. Of course, they had eventually shared this wisdom with the Moon Clan, but it would always belong to them. They had taught the good Master all he knew about the Ancient Tree Mysteries of Earth and Sky—the central focus of the Faery Wisdom Teachings.

The Faeries were not seen, however, venturing into the Realm of Men so much anymore. Because of the

Earth changes that were at hand, most chose to stay hidden deep in the Forest and beyond the Mists. Many humans over the past years, upon hearing stories of their wisdom and power, had tried to seek them out. Fortunately for the Faery Races, they were only found if they wanted to be found. Many a seeker had turned away in disappointment, for what lay within their hearts was greed and malice. They had wanted to gain access to the Records of Time stored within the rings of the trees for selfish gain. Of course, they would not have succeeded. Even if the records of the trees' rings had been accessed, they wouldn't have understood them, for they were all cast in Elyrie—the mysterious Light Language of the Trees. Alas, these misguided humans would never have been blessed with "Faery Sight." However, those with a pure heart, "ears to hear, and eyes to see" still learned a great deal from the Faery Ones; Master Ra-Ma'at marveled at their wisdom.

The part of his plan that he had not shared with Korin was this: Ra-Ma'at hoped to arrive early to the Great Gathering with ample time to spare before it commenced. He intended to have something more than his dreams to aid in the discussion. Therefore, his full plan entailed one further action step—Master Ra-Ma'at would seek entrance into the Faerie Realm. Surprisingly, this was not about his longing or desire to be with Elysinia, although he knew she would accompany him. His intentions had to do with accessing the records in the Crystal Library. His mind recalled the prophecy he had come upon long ago. He felt it might assist with understanding what lay ahead.

He also believed it might shed some light on the mysterious origin of Taivyn Green. He had begun to think that somehow, it was all connected.

He had already sent word to the other elders of the Moon Clan regarding his intent. They were dispersed throughout the land. Some of them had settled in bordering villages, preferring to live on the outskirts away from the main community. Many of them, like Lunaya, were somewhere deep in the Forest. The difference was that they often returned. His sister never did. He could not wait for them this time, though. They would have to meet him at the Great Gathering place. They, too, would have felt the invitation like a flutter within their heart. However, he wanted them to be aware of the full extent of his plan.

First thing was first—he had to find Lunaya. He knew that in order to do so, he just needed to follow the Polaris Ley Line.

Chapter 27
Gnome Hospitality

"There are fairies at the bottom of our gardens."

—Rose Fyleman (1877–1957), *"Fairies"*

The Forest – 11,000 BCE

M aster Ra-Ma'at peered at the night sky. It was beautiful, and it was dark. He wanted to get as far as possible into the Forest before making camp. He came to a small clearing easily recognized by the large yew trees that created a natural enclosure around it. These ancient "standing people," as they were often called, acted as guardians over all who lived within that clearing. As long as they were pure of heart, even outsiders were protected upon entering this space. Master Ra-Ma'at thought he remembered this particular clearing as being largely populated by tree gnomes, a family of rabbits, and the Archer Spider. Knowing them to be a hospitable bunch, he decided to settle down here for the evening.

Within no time, Ra-Ma'at had a fire kindled. He sat huddled close to it, because the night air carried with it a slight chill much better tolerated with some heat. A small figure could be seen amidst the thick root system of one of the yew trees. He materialized as if out of nowhere, but Ra-Ma'at was not surprised. He had expected one of the inhabitants to make an appearance sooner or later, as it was proper etiquette of the Forest Folk. Jory, one of the tree gnomes, came over to greet him. After a cordial exchange of salutations, Jory offered Ra-Ma'at some food.

"Sunny, could I get you something to eat? We've got some ale cakes and honey left over from supper. I'd love to share them with you!"

Ra-Ma'at produced an outer smile while grimacing to himself. He had forgotten that some of the Forest Folk referred to him in this way. They had picked it up from Lunaya, and it had stuck. He never did take to anyone besides his sister calling him Sunny. *Oh, well,* he thought to himself, *I guess old habits die hard.*

"Thanks, Jory. I, too, have some provisions that I brought with me. What do ya say we sit by the fire and break bread together?" Master Ra-Ma'at responded.

Jory's toes twinkled at that. "Why, I'd love to. You know a good gnome always eats at least seven times a day. I sure am ready for my sepper. Kids! Time for sepper!" called Jory into the tree.

"Sepper? Don't you mean supper?" asked Sunny in confusion.

"No, of course not. We already had supper. Now we are ready for sepper—our second supper! Kids!" Jory settled in next to Ra-Ma'at just as three little gnomes appeared in the hole of the tree trunk. They made their way over to where their father was sitting and plopped down. They rubbed their bellies, indicating that they, too, were ready for sepper. Ra-Ma'at chuckled to himself and began to unload his goods.

They ate their sepper silently, making sure not to miss a crumb. Then the oddly matched company stretched out to allow for proper comfort. They had been enjoying themselves by the fire for quite some time, indulging in the extra heat the embers provided, when they heard a large crash. Startled, they all turned rather abruptly to see what the source of the commotion was.

Jory and Ra-Ma'at walked carefully over toward the source of the sound. There arose from underneath a pile of leaves and dirt a long black leg. This leg did not belong to any human, however; it looked to be the leg of a rather large arachnid. Master Ra-Ma'at stared horrified. Not because of any extreme aversion to large arachnids, for he was actually quite fond of most. His horror stemmed from genuine concern for the fellow creature. Knowing that in these parts of the woods, the leg most certainly belonged to none other than the Archer Spider, Ra-Ma'at jumped to action.

"Archer Spider, is that you? Are you all right?" he called into the leaves while he dug furiously through the pile to uncover the ill-fated creature that lay beneath. Halfway through digging, he realized Jory was just standing back with his arms folded.

"Jory, what are you doing? Why aren't you helping me? The spider could be hurt. Aren't you guys friends?"

Jory did not move. Instead, the tree gnome just stood there with a somewhat reproachful look on his face. Annoyed but without time to address it, Ra-Ma'at continued digging until he was finally able to see the dejected creature. Lying on his back, the Archer Spider made a pathetic groan that begged for pity.

"Ohhhh...woe is me! Wooooeeee is me! I will never be able to climb to the moon and gather the silver thread. I'm finished I tell you. Finished!" The spider spat and snarled after his last word before dramatically tossing his eight legs back in a contrived act of capitulation. At this point, although he was quite confused, Master Ra-Ma'at found it difficult to take the Archer Spider very seriously.

He turned to Jory questioningly. "What is going on with Spider? I've never known him to be the groveling sort. And how is it that he could've fallen from a tree? Is he not a master climber and web weaver?" Ra-Ma'at was incredulous.

Jory's sigh finally broke the silence. "Well, you see, Spider here has been having a tough time. I'm not quite sure why he doesn't just give it up. He seems to have this pie in the sky idea that he needs to get to the moon. It seems this may have been another failed attempt at weaving a web that will take him there."

Master Ra-Ma'at was still not sure he understood. He turned to the spider. "But, Archer Spider, you are the greatest web weaver and climber this Forest has ever known. Why do you wish to get to the Moon?"

One of his legs was still draped over his face in disgust. "Oh, Sunny, but you don't understand. Neither of you do really."

By this time, their curiosity having gotten the best of them, the tree gnome children had crept over to where the others were. One of them, the youngest by a hundred years or so, sat upon a rock damp with mildew. He was intrigued by the whole situation, and due to his youth and the condition of his soul, he was innocent and pure. As he was clear of mind and heart and free from judgment, the rock spoke to him. Without the slightest of prompting, a vision came into his mind's eye, and he suddenly understood what the others did not. He spoke and he amazed them all.

"Father, it is important for the Archer Spider to aspire to these great heights. For even animals and Forest Folk are on their own journey of evolution. He is the greatest spider here in the Forest; it is true. However, there is always something to strive for that is greater. Grandmother Spider, who lives in the Moon and spins the Web of Life that connects us all, is the Great Teacher. She is to whom the Archer Spider does aspire. One day, I believe he will make it to the Moon and remember who he is. For now, he can do nothing else but try."

Having finished with the explanation of his profound understanding, the young one slid off the rock, and, with a childlike giggle, he scurried away.

The others were stunned speechless. They were astonished at the young tree gnome's sudden bout of wisdom. Even the Archer Spider, having relaxed his eight legs for the first time since his crash landing, sat up. For the first time since he began his journey, he felt the love and acceptance of someone who understood him. To stare into one's heart and soul and nod in understanding can sometimes be the greatest gift one can receive in a moment of difficulty.

The night continued on quite uneventfully after that. They all returned to the fire, including the Archer Spider, who enjoyed the company of the Solar Keeper whom he had not seen in quite some time. They passed the time telling tales of times past, both ancient and old. They were so engrossed in their storytelling that they did not notice the dark outsider who sat crouched behind the forest brush, watching and listening to all they said.

Chapter 28
A Traveler's Companion

"I think that at a child's birth, if a mother could ask a fairy godmother to endow it with the most useful gift, that gift should be curiosity."

—Eleanor Roosevelt

The Forest – 11,000 BCE

Taivyn looked around. He could barely see two feet ahead of him. It was so dark that he nearly tripped on some overgrown root. He would have been smart to think this through before embarking on his surreptitious journey; a little preplanning could have gone a long way. He cursed himself for being so impetuous. He bent down and felt around on the ground for his lost shoe that had flown off just seconds ago on account of the tree root. After locating it, he continued on.

At this point, he had no idea in which direction the Master had gone. He squinted and believed he could make out a dim glow in the distance. Then again, his eyes could just as easily have been playing tricks on him. He had been wandering for hours. For a while, he was certain he was hot on the Master's trail. Taivyn must have taken a wrong turn, though, because he had not heard footsteps or seen any sign of Master Ra-Ma'at for at least an hour. Taivyn was not accustomed to the pitch black, and he certainly did not know anything about traveling alone in the Forest, least of all at night.

He was feeling at a loss and near ready to turn around and retrace his steps back to the community when he saw something move. Seeing perhaps was not an accurate way to describe the sensation that he experienced just then—it was more like he felt someone—or something—else there with him. It was an unfamiliar and dark *presence*. He felt a shiver run up his spine. He contemplated making a dash for it. That's when the faint light he thought he had detected up ahead became indisputable. Now he was positively sure of it. He hurriedly made his way toward the light, hoping to elude whatever it was in the Forest with him. As he got closer to the source of illumination, he observed he was on the edge of a clearing; it was a natural enclosure of ancient trees. He could not identify the particular species, because he had not yet made it to the subject of Tree Lore and Wisdom in his studies. He cautiously approached the edge of the clearing now, close enough to discern that the light was coming from a campfire.

He spotted the Master huddled up next to the flames. Next, he observed that the Master was not alone. He had company. Taivyn gasped. He could not believe his eyes. The Master was not only sitting in the company of a rather large spider but also with a family of tree gnomes. At least he thought they were probably tree gnomes from all the descriptions he had heard. Taivyn had not actually ever encountered a tree gnome before now; tree gnomes were only something that one might run into on long adventures in the Forest, which the Master had always been against Taivyn having.

Taivyn crept in quietly; he wanted to get as close as possible so he could better hear what they were talking about. The Master was speaking.

"There is something that is troubling me beyond what started me on this quest. When I left the community, I heard a very distinct sound just before entering into the Forest. I had never actually heard the sound before now. When I heard it, however, I was sure I knew what it was. It was just like all the books and records have always said—that one's heart would recognize the sound."

The tree gnomes sat deeply engrossed. If they knew to what the Master was alluding, they did nothing to indicate that such was the case. The spider, however, was not impressed, "Yes, yes, of course—the Crossing of the Frog and the Mushroom is at hand."

Chapter 29

A Spider Weaves a Tale:
The Frog and The Mushroom

*"Storytelling is a very old form of hypnosis and
as such is a powerful tool for transformation."*

—Thea Summer Deer, *Wisdom
of the Plant Devas*

The Forest – 11,000 BCE

The young tree gnomes had never heard about the
Crossing of the Frog and the Mushroom before. It
was a tale their father did not dare speak of even now.
Jory interjected rather abruptly, "All right, children, it is
getting late. It is probably time to be heading off into
the tree for some much needed rest. Come now."

Noticing their father's quick change in temperament
further ignited their inquiring little minds. "Aww. But,
Father, we haven't even had trinner yet or a cup of tea.
Let the spider tell us the legend. He always weaves the
best stories. Come on, Pa. Can we, huh? Can we?"

Outnumbered, Jory grumbled with distaste. Perhaps his worries were unfounded. Maybe it could do him well to hear the story once again. It had been almost half a millennium since he last heard it told. What could be the harm in a little legend telling? He conceded. "Oh, all right! Fine. But then it's off to sleep!"

The fire crackled. The golden light danced with the trees as it reflected off the seemingly black leaves above. The spider smiled happily, content to weave a spellbinding tale. Thus he began.

"The frog lives in a magical realm that exists in many places at once. Here we see him jumping between lily pads. The lily pad he jumps on determines which world he may appear in that day. The frog loves the company of the mushroom. To us, the mushroom may be nothing more than interesting fungi. We may look and say, 'What an intriguing form that is!' or we may even exclaim, 'My, what beautiful colors and designs it has!' To the frog, however, the mushroom is so much more; it is his friend and his companion. When they speak to one another, their dialogue creates a song that even the bluebirds stop to listen to for a while. In the world of man, the mushrooms is a stationary form, but in the Forest, he is anything but. He moves around as he pleases. He was given the gift of movement from a faery as payment for a debt owed many aeons ago, but that is another story.

"The mushroom is very wise. Many do not know the mushroom for his wisdom, however. The frog is the only one who truly knows and understands this extraordinary aspect of the mushroom's nature.

Regardless of being misunderstood, the mushroom is a jovial creature and gets on quite well with most creatures of the Forest, particularly the gnomes."

At this the spider paused momentarily and glanced at the young tree gnomes to calculate their level of interest. Just as he had suspected, they were mesmerized and hanging on his every word. Even Jory was intensely focused. The light of the fire made his eyes appear as two kaleidoscopes side by side. Pleased at the effect his story was having, he continued weaving the enchanting tale.

"'Why is the relationship of the frog and the mushroom so special?' you ask. Well, in truth, there are as many versions to the story, and answers to that question, as there are stars in the sky above. Perhaps we will never completely understand the truth. Perhaps the truth, in this case, is unimportant. It was told to me once long ago that the mushroom is a regal creature and magical in nature akin to the Faery kingdom, cousins if you will, although they were not always acting family members.

"The mushroom is quite unlike any creature known to man. Even to 'those with eyes to see,' he may still appear static upon first glance. Shortly thereafter, you will see, though, that he is not stationary at all—he moves! The mushroom has eyes to assess what is before him, as he is very calculating, not in a sly and clever way but in a very strategic way, you see. And his movements reflect this way of being. He never makes a move unless he is completely committed. When he does move, it is most definite indeed. Mushroom moves according to the shade of the moon, the sound of the wind through the trees, the croak of the locust. Of course, he will tell you that moving in this way is very mathematical and makes perfect sense. I don't dare argue.

"Because of all this, when he moves, it is an act of power! You see, the mushroom is on a long journey. The journey is not something that we could ever really grasp. It is an internal journey reflected in his outer movements. He can move in one place for years, or he can travel great distances at the speed of light, give or take units, but always will his steps be based on truth. When you trace back his movements over time, you will see it is like a map. But only the frog truly understands this language, and that is why they are fellow pilgrims. They do not travel together, but they do, upon meeting, commune in a way that is inconceivable even to the deftest of souls. Whenever the frog and the mushroom cross paths, a great conjunction occurs. The moment of the crossing itself is a time for joy and celebration, for it creates a powerful opportunity indeed. The crossing is like a key to a long-forgotten map; with it one can decipher and utilize all the power in the mushroom's movements up until that point. It can become a wonderful tool for transformation and awakening by one who is able to harness its power."

Jory interrupted abruptly. "Who needs power like that? The power that can be derived from the event of their crossing is raw and unchecked. It could split a hole in the fabric of creation itself, creating an act of pure antilife! No, thank you! Not me! We would be fools to meddle with such things!"

Jory had finished his tirade. The others concurred with this. However, if one passed up all the opportunities that could have a potential negative outcome, one might never do anything worth doing.

Taivyn was so excited he nearly fell over. He must have made too audible of a sound, because the spider looked over in his direction. He ducked, hoping he had not been discovered. He collected himself and peeked around the large yew tree. The spider had turned his attention back to the conversation.

"One would think that this occurrence happened quite frequently. Alas, it does not. For in truth, there is only one frog and one mushroom. The others are only holographic illusions, a memory, a magical clue about this uncanny event."

The spider had entranced everyone with his story. Woven with the grace of a skilled dancer, of which only he was ever capable, the spider was truly the first bard. Really, all the bards would learn the seductive art of storytelling from the spider, but that would be getting ahead of oneself. To say Taivyn was captivated would have been a great understatement; he was mesmerized. He could not believe he had never heard this beguiling tale told before. He knew it must be the prophecy about which the Master had spoken of to Korin. Furthermore, he knew he had to find this frog and mushroom. It was surely his destiny. Of course, for what purpose, he was unsure. But, clearly, this must pertain to him.

Taivyn was too busy getting over himself to notice when exactly it was that the dark *presence* had caught up to him. When he did become aware, however, he froze with terror. It felt as if it were closing in on him. He started to panic. He hunkered down into a ball and sat there, shaking in his bones. A howl was heard in the distance. That was when someone or something swooped in and plucked him up by his tunic.

He started wailing. "Let me go! You dark and decrepit creature of the night! Let me go! I am a powerful wizard. When I get a hold of you, you will be sorry you ever messed with me! Let me go!"

All the while, he had been kicking and swinging as he dangled in the air with his eyes closed. He did not dare open them, for fear of what might be facing him.

"Taivyn!" He was too busy screaming and flailing about to notice that whatever it was, man or beast, it knew his name.

"What are you doing here!" it asked in a chiding tone. Instantly, Taivyn snapped out of it, because he recognized the familiar voice. He decided to peel one of his eyelids open to confirm. A gush of relief washed over him. It was the Master who had apprehended him. Then reality set it. Drat! He'd been found, and from the vexed grimace on the Master's face, he was not terribly pleased.

The Master set Taivyn down somewhat gruffly. A rush of thoughts ran through him then, and the young boy quickly forgot about the original cause for his fear. He was too concerned with figuring out how to explain himself that he did not even think to mention *the dark presence* he had felt. Every excuse he thought of in that two-second interval sounded ridiculous. There was no way out of it.

"I, I, I…well, it's hard to explain, Master. I…I…I just wanted to help!" he blurted out. There he had said it. He watched the Master's face very closely. He was hoping that he would lighten up soon. That desire was not fulfilled.

"You what? Taivyn, I really don't understand! Why did you do this? What do you mean you wanted to help? How did you find me?" Ra-Ma'at was floored. He just could not believe Taivyn had followed him here. What in the world had the boy been thinking?

Taivyn attempted to answer his Master's line of questioning but was quickly shushed. "Never mind for now. First thing's first: we need to get you warmed up. You are chilled to the bone. Why don't you join us by the fire?"

Taivyn had not realized he was shivering. The night's cold must have set in. The two of them walked over to where the others were gathered. The tree gnomes who had been eavesdropping quickly turned their attention back to the fire. There was a tension in the air that made them very uncomfortable; tree gnomes hated tension (this was probably why they did not get along with most of the bog wights who were known to be the tensest creatures in the Forest). They did not quite understand why everyone could not just get along and eat. After all, it worked for them.

Pretending not to have heard anything that had transpired between Ra-Ma'at and the boy, Jory offered,

"Well, hello there. What might your name be? Are you a fellow traveler of Sunny's? Glad you could join us. We were just about to brew some tea. We will be starting on trinner soon."

Jory smiled and gestured to his children who were pointing to their opened mouths, indicating their intention to eat again. He placed some green and reddish brown herbs into a pot of water and hung it over the fire. Master Ra-Ma'at handed Taivyn a blanket and pointed at a pile of leaves, indicating Taivyn should be seated—next to the spider! The Archer Spider continued where he had left off as if nothing had happened.

"So, you see, the signs are clear. If indeed the Time of the Frog and the Mushroom has come once again, then not only is a new age upon us, but we are on the brink of something significant. This conjunction is something that has not happened for aeons, according to the Records of Time. And I can assure you this crossing has not occurred yet, but when it does, there will be a chance to envision something greater than we have ever conceived of before! Which is why I must continue to try to get to the Moon—I have an opportunity to become a Grandmother Spider."

Not really comprehending the spiritual evolutionary path of a spider, Ra-Ma'at asked for clarity. "So you are saying the next step in your spiritual development is to become a grandmother spider. Archer Spider, forgive me, but I was always under the impression that you were a male. Now call me crazy, but I thought…"

The spider interrupted quickly, understanding where Ra-Ma'at was going. "Yes, I am male per se, but the only example we have of a fully realized spider being is 'Grandmother Spider,' so that is to whom I aspire. That being said, I would have no objections to being a Grandfather Spider if that is indeed where the path led me."

Satisfied with his explanation, the spider sat back in repose. Ra-Ma'at relented, as he had never heard of another full spider being apart from the Grandmother Spider either. Taivyn mused that perhaps he and the spider had more in common than he had originally perceived. His respect for this arachnid was growing exponentially.

The tea was ready, and Jory offered Taivyn a cup. The tea gave off a stench that could only be attributed to stinkberry and bur. Taivyn was not really excited about the malodorous liquid, but he was smart enough to know better than to insult a gnome.

Ra-Ma'at did not waste any time. As soon as Taivyn was comfortable and thawing out, he began his line of questioning again. Taivyn hesitated before answering. He thought about lying, but then decided against it. No, he had to tell the truth. He started from the beginning. More out of shame than fear of punishment, Taivyn cringed as he told the Master the part about having overheard his conversation with Korin. He explained his resolution to follow the Master into the Forest. He knew it was wrong, and that it went against all the values of the Moon Clan, which Taivyn had spent so much time learning. He left in search of answers, but his intentions were pure in that he really had thought he could help.

As angry and irritated as Master Ra-Ma'at was with Taivyn for his blatant act of disobedience, he could not help but empathize. He knew that the boy's curiosity was unchecked, but at the same time, he knew it was what drove him. If channeled properly, it could be a very powerful catalyst for something great—exactly the type of great that the prophecy within the crystal had foretold. Still, this was not a time for leniency.

The long silence that followed Taivyn's recounting of his story kept the boy on edge. He knew he had messed up. He knew Master Ra-Ma'at was considering all he had said. When Ra-Ma'at finally spoke, Taivyn was almost relieved.

"Taivyn, I cannot say that I am pleased with your behavior or the choices you've made. While I do not fault you for your burning desire for exploration and understanding, I do feel you have gone too far in this case. I am inclined to forgive you; however, you must not continue on. It is too dangerous out here for a young boy; furthermore, I cannot be slowed down in my quest. Tomorrow, at first light, you will start back for the community. I am sorry you have come all this way, but it is a lesson well learned I hope."

Taivyn started to object. He had not come all this way just to turn around and go home. The community. Bah! There was nothing going on there. This was where all the action was. What was the old wizard talking about? Hadn't the Master heard anything he had said?

"Besides, what about the prophecy?" Taivyn questioned.

Master Ra-Ma'at winced. He had forgotten that he had spoken about the prophecy to Korin. Taivyn must have heard that as well. "Taivyn, listen to me. There are no guarantees where prophecies are concerned. Mostly, we don't even know what they are referring to until it is upon us. I said that to Korin to give him something to chew on for the time being."

Taivyn was not convinced. "You mean you lied? I doubt that. I know it must have something to do with me being an orphan. Do you know where I came from? Or who my parents are? Nobody seems to want to say it out loud, but I can say it: I'm an orphan who was abandoned for some reason, maybe because they didn't love me. It's okay. You don't have to say it. I know I don't fit in at the community. It's because I am not of the Moon Clan. That couldn't be more obvious!"

As much as Taivyn was trying to put on a tough act, Ra-Ma'at knew better. He knew that underneath it all, Taivyn had a sensitive and tender heart, which was easily hurt. His fearless façade was a defense mechanism that usually worked with most people. There was no fooling the Master, though. Unfortunately, Ra-Ma'at did not have many answers for Taivyn where his birth parents or origin were concerned. He had been very forthcoming about what he did know. He felt deep sympathy for the boy.

"Taivyn, I am so sorry that I do not have more answers for you about where you came from. I have told you mostly everything I know about the circumstances of your arrival."

Ra-Ma'at recalled the day Taivyn was brought to him sixteen years ago. An emissary from the Faeries arrived that day. He carried with him a baby nestled inside a woven basket, along with the letter signed in moonlight by the Council of Five, specifically Elysinia. It was the first word Ra-Ma'at had received from her since her departure. She did not say much except that the baby had come to her, and it was very important that he be well cared for and brought up in the ways of the Moon Clan people. Wanting to fulfill his beloved's request, Ra-Ma'at saw to the boy's instruction from day one.

"What about the frog and the mushroom?" Taivyn inquired innocently.

Exhausted from this futile argument, the Master answered finally, "Taivyn, the frog and the mushroom have nothing to do with you. It is an event of power; one that you have no business interfering with."

"I know there is a prophecy out there that pertains to me, and I'm going to find it!" Taivyn yelled in the bratty tone of a rebellious teenager.

"Then you should have stayed back at the community and looked into it, along with Korin! You won't find any answers out here. There is nothing for you here—only danger and uncertainty!"

The Master was losing his patience. There was no time for this. There was much at stake, and, as much as he did not want to brush Taivyn aside, the boy needed to understand that this was not just about him. This was about all of them. They could all be in grave danger, especially if the time had truly come for the Crossing of the Frog and the Mushroom. As the spider mentioned, the conjunction could be seen as a great opportunity if harnessed properly—perhaps they could even work with the power generated by that event to somehow preserve the sacred teachings. The conjunction itself would have to be crystal recorded to utilize it as a key.

Ra-Ma'at thought of Maob, one of the Moon Clan elders who had been tasked to chart the movements of the mushroom. Of course, like a keyless map, these movements were meaningless without the illumination given by the point of crossing. It was only in the crossing that the power in the movements could be activated and used one way or another. However, if that power were to fall into the wrong hands...Ra-Ma'at shuddered at the possibility.

Master Ra-Ma'at had made up his mind. He repeated his decision firmly. "Taivyn, you will return home tomorrow. That is an order. There is nothing else to be said about the situation."

Taivyn folded his arms and wore the most stubborn expression of which he was capable. If the Master was not going to allow Taivyn to accompany him on his journey, he would just have to go on a quest of his own. There was no way he was going back to the community without some answers.

Chapter 30
It Was by My Mother's Garden

*"The nature of infinity is this: That everything
has its own vortex, and when once a traveler
through Eternity has pass'd that Vortex, he
perceives it roll backward behind his path, into
a globe itself unfolding like a sun..."*

—William Blake, *"Milton"*

Maine – 2004

Jedda was jubilant. She felt like she was walking on
rainbows. No, she was hopping, bouncing, skipping
joyfully on them. She had to think, but then again she
didn't. For the first time in a long time, Jedda did not
have anything to think about, because she felt it. Her
whole being sang in resonance to the truths that were
discussed earlier that evening with Lou and Isis. Like a
wide-eyed little girl on Christmas morning, Jedda felt
the magic and wonder that pervades many a childhood.

She allowed herself the indulgence of reminiscing
about the past. Her mind floated back to an image

when she was four or five years old. She had this distinctly vivid memory of strolling through her mother's gardens. That was where everything had made sense for her.

To say that her mother had a green thumb was a great understatement. Diane Delaney had a natural ability to grow anything. She could probably have grown a coral reef in a desert if she had tried. Her gardens had always resembled faery playgrounds. Everything appeared wild and grown out. Roses grew on the fence, and marigolds popped out of nowhere. A lilac bush here, a hibiscus tree there. Nothing was out of place, and yet nothing looked landscaped by human hands. It couldn't have been better planned if the Earth were left to her own devices. It was as if they had a daily powwow, Mother Earth and her mom, whereby they drew up their plans to create the most beautiful, wild, and natural garden setting that ever was.

This was the opposite of an English garden. There were no manicured lawns or patterns of similar flowers. This was not a blue-bells-and-cocker-shells-nicely-in-a-row garden. This was a free-flowing masterpiece, a divine garden where faeries and angels played. Her mother co-created with nature every day, and she didn't even consciously know it. Of course, on some very deep level, her mother must have known.

Jedda recalled the feeling that she experienced during these garden meanderings. A desire to know the world would rise up, and along with it a profound yearning to connect with some long-forgotten part of herself. The universe was a magical place then, where possibilities were endless and the requests of the heart were listened to and answered. She remembered being part of that universe; in fact, it had been so deeply woven into the foundation of her reality then that she had felt akin to the stars and the moon. How could she have forgotten this? It came floating back to her in a bubble that seemed to originate from another lifetime.

She had known that magic existed without a shadow of a doubt. When did she abandon that knowing and why? Somehow she had forgotten. She vowed to never forget again. Jedda reached for her journal to record her impressions and emotions. Jarringly, she was brought back to the aggravating recollection that her little brother had thieved it. She pondered confronting him and decided against it. She was in a state of peacefulness that she did not want interrupted. For a while, she continued to allow her mind to wander down memory lane. Then she returned to the present. She thought about all that Lou had shared with her. Being a school night they had run out of time, and had not even begun to discuss the meaning of the symbol yet. Jedda was ecstatic over the notion of another meeting with her teacher who had assured her would be very soon. Lou had said that she wanted to give Jedda some time to allow all the new information to percolate. Jedda grinned at the image that word conjured—one of those old English teapots beginning to boil over.

Jedda was imbued with a new sense of purpose. A Keeper. She did not know what that really entailed, but for some reason, she was not afraid of assuming this responsibility, whatever it was. In the past, Jedda had shirked away from taking on extra commitments that would have kept her from the activities she loved, such as reading, writing, being outdoors. This did not feel like she would have to give up anything at all. Instead, it felt like a homecoming, as if her life were fuller because of it.

If she for one minute allowed her left-brain to catch up to her right-brain, she was sure she would hear the familiar naysayer screaming that all this was a crock, and that it was highly implausible. That was exactly why she did not let it get the better of her. Writing was not really an option right now for reasons she did not want to dwell on, namely, that her journal was missing. She decided to take a walk outside. It was not yet too late, and Jedda could use the fresh air.

She threw a jacket on and went for a stroll. She walked and walked, admiring the gift of nature. She heard a few night birds making chirping sounds. She strolled down the driveway and down the narrow winding path that led to the end of the street. She breathed in the crisp night air and felt refreshed. There was the comfort of trees all around. Only the evergreens still had green left on their branches from the needles that they did not shed even in these often subzero temperatures. She looked up. How high they were. Some of them looked like they were trying to grow toward the stars.

After twenty minutes or so, she started to make her return back down the winding narrow street to the edge of her driveway. The driveway was dotted by small shrubs and bushes, and, of course, the willow tree. She felt it welcome her home. She knelt down on the cold concrete momentarily. She wanted to give herself a second to look up in its branches. A part of her hoped to see the raven, for she believed that she was ready for the journey that lay ahead. Remembering. That's what he had called it—a journey of remembering.

She started to move out of her kneeling position when a flickering light over one of the smaller bushes caught her eye. So as not to disturb it, she remained poised and seated. Jedda tilted her head to get a better view. The light appeared to be a glowing bauble no larger than her palm. It floated in her direction and stopped a few inches from her nose, which was where it hovered fleetingly.

Jedda blinked once, then twice. Her rational mind wanted to explain it away and say that it was nothing more than a lightning bug; however, her common sense told her that the lightning bug theory was an impossibility, seeing as it was March in Maine. Clearly, it was way too early for a firefly appearance, not to mention it was way too cold. Perhaps this was one of the glowworms about which she had read.

"Right, Jedda! Snap out of it!" she reprimanded herself. "Glowworms are worms. They wouldn't be flying above your nose!"

Too much pressure on the mind can cause it to short-circuit. And that was exactly what happened next. Jedda's mind doubled back on itself, like a brain flip-flop, and then it was gone—not the glowing orb, but her thoughts. Jedda was having a total eclipse of the mind where the only thing that remained was the Silence. The mind had no explanation for what was occurring. When her rational mind collapsed, an opening within her occurred. Suddenly everything in the entire universe made sense. It was in that moment that Jedda Rose Delaney knew she was witnessing a faery in flight.

Jedda rubbed her eyes just to be sure, but when that did not change what fluttered before her, she conceded. She remembered her childhood, and how she had always wished they would appear to her. She had been, after all, one of the only people left in the whole world besides her mother who still believed in them. Before today, they never had appeared to her. Eventually, she had given up wishing.

Here, as if in delayed answer to her unspoken desire all those years ago, the little light being floated so daintily before her. It twirled around and started floating away from her. Jedda finally unfurled her legs from her tucked position on the ground and rose. She started to follow it. Then instantly, as if it knew her intention, it circled back toward her. Before too long, it was joined by two more glowing lights. Tears gathered in Jedda's eyes. Her heart was bursting asunder with love and gratitude for what she knew and felt in that moment but could not describe. Being splashed with Faery Light can have that effect on someone.

Suddenly, she understood at a very deep level their relationship to her and All That Is. She understood their role in the Web of Life and saw how they helped everything come into form and grow. Jedda knew this was all part of some greater plan. It had to be.

The faery lights were twinkling on and off now, as if trying to draw her attention to something. They floated over to where the willow tree grew. Jedda stood before the tree and peered at its sweeping branches that swayed in the wind. The light of the moon cast its shadow upon the driveway, giving the impression that it was immense in size. Jedda drew closer to this favorite tree of hers. She turned around and pressed her back up against its trunk and breathed. One of the faery lights glided upward, and then the willow's branches became alive and glittered with hundreds of these faery orbs. Jedda could feel them all, as if they were one. It was both mystical and natural at the same time. She could feel the sap moving within the tree and wondered if it were her imagination. Images began to pour into her mind, but she did not understand what they meant. They were moving fast like files opening one after another. Afraid of what was happening, Jedda pulled away from the tree. Her heart was racing, and her mind was confused and unsorted. What was happening to her?

She fell upon the ground, and for the first time since she was a little girl, Jedda began to pray.

"Universe! Because that is what God is anyway, isn't it? She? He? I know we haven't talked in a while, but I think maybe now is as good a time as ever. Please. Please. Please! Help me to understand what's happening to me. Please help me. This seems all so magnificent, but some of it is very scary, too. I'm not sure what to do. And these images frighten me. I don't understand. If someone is trying to get some message across to me—I don't understand! It felt like I tapped into some infinite spring of wisdom where all information is stored. How can this be? Help me please!"

Tears were streaming down her face now, and Jedda was in complete and total surrender. The moonlight made her tears look like little rivers of silver light. Just then the faery lights began to dim, and something started to move within the tree trunk. A light from within the tree began to shine forth and illuminate a doorway once again. She recognized the vesica piscis that lay encrusted on the surface and marked the entranceway that she had passed through the week before.

She looked upward at the sky and wondered if this were an answer to her prayer. She looked around and then approached cautiously. She knocked as she had learned to do and stepped back to allow the passageway to open. For the second time, Jedda proceeded through the tree portal. With nothing but a grain of faith and a feeling that said, "The answers you are seeking are within," Jedda stepped into the unknown.

Chapter 31
Peace of Mind

"The indescribable vibration of the heart
spreads into every center of your sacred body
temple, revealing to your astonished
consciousness all the hidden jewels which were
veiled to sight before."

—Ruby Nelson, *The Door of Everything*

The Forest – 11,000 BCE

Master Ra-Ma'at sat upon a large granite rock just beyond the clearing. He could feel the rock's vibration as it pulsed through his body and soothed his mind. He allowed himself to feel the comfort of this pulsating life-force energy. It helped him to let go a little bit. Then he centered himself and plunged deep into the expansiveness of his being to feel and remember.

What was it that was bothering him? Then, like a lightning bolt, an understanding flashed from deep within. He began to recall a time when he was just a young boy starting out on his chosen path. He looked deeper and saw Taivyn there, alone and misunderstood. Ra-Ma'at could identify with him, because he had felt this way often in his young life. His only saving grace had been his dear twin sister who had often felt the same. They, at least, had each other to share this lonely path. Taivyn did not have the respite that came from the unconditional love of a sibling, or family for that matter.

He continued to observe what he was noticing and feeling. Then, suddenly, he saw the answer before him so clearly. He knew that everything was connected, and there were no coincidences in the universe. Nothing had been an accident—not Taivyn following him or being there, not Ra-Ma'at sitting upon that rock. He couldn't believe it! It had been staring him in the face the whole time, and he had been blind to it.

He still felt a little guilty over the way he had reacted to Taivyn. He had been way too harsh with the boy, not just this evening, but as of late. It was like a part of him had wanted to shut the boy out to protect him from what might very well be his destiny. He acknowledged the guilt and forgave himself. He wasn't perfect, and there was always room for improvement.

He opened his eyes and looked into the small tree enclosure in front of him. The fizzling campfire had died down now to glowing embers that crackled and popped sporadically. He looked at his fellow companions curled up on the ground. The three youngin' gnomes had convinced Jory to let them sleep outside of the tree tonight. He had begrudgingly agreed to it. They slept now soundly, huddled up to one another. From where Ra-Ma'at sat, it looked like a colorful pile of hair and clothes.

Then he glanced over at the Archer Spider, who appeared calm and serene in his slumber. It must have been a great relief for him to have the gift of understanding bestowed upon him. The young tree gnome had given him that. Ra-Ma'at recalled the look of comfort on the spider's face when the tree gnome had revealed the spider's deepest, innermost dreams and aspirations, as if he himself were the one aspiring to such heights. What solace understanding can bring!

He finally looked over at Taivyn nestled in a small blue blanket that the gnomes had managed to manifest (for gnomes are magnificent manifesters, second only to leprechauns). He knew then what Taivyn must have felt, not just tonight but always. It was the feeling of aloneness one feels that comes with being misunderstood. And that was an unfortunate way to live one's life.

Ra-Ma'at was resolved. He knew that he would not send Taivyn back to the community the next day. There was nowhere Taivyn felt more misunderstood than there. It wasn't that everyone in the Moon Clan wasn't nice to the boy, because they were. They all tried very hard to make him feel welcome. It was a constant reminder, though, that he was different, and that he was an orphan. No one understood where he had come from or why the Faery Emissary had brought him to the community. After a while, everyone just accepted that it was one of the mysteries of working with the Faery Ones. He never really fit in, though.

Taivyn was just a teenage boy, but he wasn't stupid. In fact, he was too smart for his own good. The Master smiled. He had taught the boy well considering all the circumstances. Well, it was decided that he would not shut Taivyn out. He would not be the cause of the boy going astray. If sent back to the community, Taivyn might be fine in the short run, but he would feel compelled to act out eventually. Who knows? There was no guarantee that the boy would even return to the community. He had, after all, come this far. No, the choice was obvious. Master Ra-Ma'at would invite Taivyn to remain with him on his quest. That was the only right thing to do. Besides, if everything were really all connected—Taivyn, the prophecy, the dreams, perhaps even the frog and the mushroom—then the safest place for Taivyn to be was under Master Ra-Ma'at's supervision.

Chapter 32
A Decision for Better or for Worse

"Nature speaks in symbols and in signs."

—John Greenleaf Whittier

The Forest – 11,000 BCE

It was really late. Nature's night sonata played in the background as they dreamt. The sound of an owl hooting echoed off the trees, making it difficult to know from where the large bird of prey hailed.

Taivyn's dreams were consumed by an image of a red rose. He reached out his hand to take the rose, and then he awoke. He peeled one eyelid open to see if it was morning yet. Still dark. He thought about what the Master had said. He needed to make a decision. He could slip away unseen into the Night Forest. Of course, it would be obvious to everyone when they all awoke, but at least he'd have a decent head start.

Alternatively, he could wait it out until morning when the Master intended to send him away. He could pretend to go back, but then, once he had gone far enough, he could change course and head in another direction. One thing was for sure: he was not returning to the Moon Clan community. Not now. Maybe not ever. It was time. He needed answers about who he was and where he had come from.

Taivyn thought long and hard about his two options. They were both well-formulated plans in his opinion; however, for some reason unbeknownst to him, he chose the former. The last thing he wanted to do was upset the Master, although somewhere deep down maybe he craved the Master's attention and recognition. He wanted to be seen. That was perhaps all he had ever wanted.

And so, without any more deliberation, Taivyn Green quietly wiggled out of his blanket and slid away into the depths of the Night Forest.

Taivyn made his way through the woods. He walked, stumbled, and tripped through the night. Brambles and thorns ripped at his clothing, making his garments tattered and torn, befitting of a true orphan. Unseen things of the night grabbed and pulled on him. His fear was great, but his determination was greater. When the first light of the morning sun began to peak through the foliage, Taivyn breathed a sigh of relief. He took it as an invitation for respite and collapsed out of sheer exhaustion. The Forest floor was moist from the morning dew. The last thing he saw was a scene of multicolored patches before he closed his eyes to rest.

◆ ◆ ◆

The morning came all too soon. Ra-Ma'at stretched his arms and back as he greeted the rays of sunlight that trickled in through the forest canopy. He welcomed the gift of warmth that these sunbeams carried to him this morning. He rubbed his neck to work out any discomfort that might be there as a result of sleeping on the forest floor. He started to rise. The anticipation of the journey to come was upon him. He looked around and saw the gnomes. A feather floated above Jory's mouth and rose into the air with every exhalation—a good indication that they were still deep in sleep. The spider was reclining all his eight legs upon a small boulder rock. He didn't move when Ra-Ma'at got up, and so it was determined that he, too, was still asleep.

Then that all-too-familiar lightning bolt struck Ra-Ma'at once again. He appeared dumbstruck, as if hit by some unexpected blow. His eyes scanned the spot where Taivyn had been lying asleep the night before. Only a crumpled blue blanket remained. Master Ra-Ma'at howled a sigh of defeat. He had failed, because he knew that Taivyn Green was gone.

Chapter 33
A Rose by Any Other Name

"Nobody sees a flower, really, it is so small. We haven't time—and to see takes time like to have a friend takes time."

—Georgia O'Keeffe

The Forest – 11,000 BCE

Taivyn must have fallen asleep, because the next thing that happened was another series of dreams. He dreamt of faeries and dragons. And somewhere in the darkness of his dream, there again was a rose.

When Taivyn awoke, he found himself surrounded by a mist. He couldn't see in front of him. His hands and feet were completely obscured. It was no longer dark; night had come and gone. The morning must have brought with it this mist rising up as if from nowhere. He started to pat the ground around him to get his bearings. That's when he heard it—a song so enchanting that it made his heart skip a beat. It was a dreamy liquid voice that reminded him of something.

There were no words, but the melody was intoxicating and sweet beyond his wildest dreams. He was spellbound.

As suddenly as it had arisen, the mist began to dissipate and give way to the scene of beauty that was before him. He had come to a flower-filled meadow, a dazzling sight for the eyes to behold. There were bright splashes of color everywhere, as if creating an intricately woven tapestry. The colors were so vivid, so vibrant, that Taivyn nearly lost his breath as he took it all in. Never once had Taivyn seen splendor such as this.

The meadow was dotted with trees here and there. Long wispy grass shoots appeared in between. Green moss grew all over the rocks and tree trunks, making everything look magical. A winged creature fluttered by his nose, causing a tickle, which he quickly brushed away. Taivyn looked around and admired the majesty before him.

Then he heard the song again. He heard it, but he knew not from where it came. He stood still, waiting to see if he could sense the point of origin.

"I suppose you've never heard the rose's song before."

Startled, Taivyn jumped. He turned around. No one was there. He turned again, and the voice said, "Over here. I believe you are looking for me."

"Where are you? I can't see you," Taivyn said.

"That's because you are looking in all the wrong places," said the voice so sweetly. "Look down."

He did as she instructed, and then he saw her—a red rose, the color of a ruby's kiss. As he gazed at the flower, he became lost in her beauty. A golden wave of light seemed to descend upon him. He became entranced and yet consciously aware of what was happening. A recollection tugged on him. He felt separated from it, though, by some impenetrable abyss. What was this memory?

"Was it you that was singing?" he asked the rose. Suddenly, he felt a little funny. Since when do roses, or any flowers for that matter, talk? Yet he could not take his eyes away from her. The song, the voice, and the rose were enrapturing. It stirred something within him buried so deep that he didn't know it had even existed until now. The rose continued her song, as if in answer to his question.

"It is you! You were the one singing!" Taivyn almost screamed in amazement. He was sure he saw the rose's color deepen a shade or two just then.

"All flowers have a song if you stop to listen," and with that she continued singing.

"What about what I feel—I can't describe it. I feel golden waves of light dancing all around me and within me, too!" Taivyn was elated.

"Haven't you ever been kissed by a rose before? Obviously not, judging by your expression," the rose answered.

"I'm sorry?" Taivyn was confused. What did she mean? "I don't understand. I guess I've never heard a flower sing before. A flower has never spoken to me before now."

The rose responded, "A shame really. Why, you probably just have never stopped to listen."

Taivyn was at a loss for words. He was stunned that he was experiencing a flower speaking, especially to him. And that voice. It was a song that reminded him of some home that he didn't realize he had until then.

"So tell me, boy. What brings you so deep into the Forest? We don't often see young boys trotting about, you know. I sang that song especially for you."

"Really?" Now it was Taivyn's turn to blush. Once he realized he was blushing, he quickly turned around to conceal his embarrassment. "Well...it's sort of a long story, but the short version is that I am on a sort of quest."

"Oh, I see." The rose tried to sound impressed.

"Yes, and, well...I'm not entirely sure I've made the best decision about it, but really, I felt like I didn't have a choice. You see, I am on a quest to find out who I am and where I come from. Hopefully, that will help me to know where I belong. And maybe, just maybe, I can find the frog and the mushroom and help my Master."

The rose appeared slightly agitated about this but tried to appear disinterested. "The frog and the mushroom. Ah, I see. Why do you search for the frog and the mushroom?"

"Because I think that somehow it will help my Master. I think he seeks them. And, ultimately, he is the only person who really cares for me or understands me. I have to help him."

"Well, many questers have sought the power that comes from the Crossing of the Frog and the Mushroom. Most cannot handle that kind of power, though. With that power comes a great deal of responsibility. You see the power is great. It is unrivaled in its magnitude, but that isn't all. One must be able to wield it properly. By properly, I mean for the good of the whole. If not, it can cause great suffering."

Taivyn thought about all the rose had said. He knew she was right. What did he know about some frog and mushroom? He had to admit he had no idea what he was doing. He became downtrodden. The rose noticed his change in attitude. She offered, "Listen to me closely, boy. Sometimes we search for things outside of ourselves to distract us from looking within. Humans tend to get big ideas about attaining something that doesn't really matter. There is only here and now. All the answers you could ever seek are within you. I believe you will find out who you are. Only you can choose your path to knowing. I will sing a song that will help you."

And with that the rose continued her song again. This time, though, the song had a slightly different quality to it. It evoked a strange sensation in Taivyn's soul of timelessness. He surrendered to the sound and let himself be carried by the wings of the otherworldly notes.

Chapter 34
Nowhere to Be Found

*"Ancient man contained within his mightly
limbs all things of heaven and earth."*

—William Blake, Chosen Chief of the Druids
Order from 1799–1827

The Forest – 11,000 BCE

Master Ra-Ma'at wandered around the Forest in
search of Taivyn for the better part of the
morning. He could have gone anywhere. He wouldn't
have gone back in the direction of the community for
sure, but other than that, it was anyone's guess.

"I don't know about you, but I'm hungry!"

It was Jory. He had decided to accompany Sunny on
his quest. He especially wanted to help him find the
boy. Jory liked the boy and admired his bravery. He
didn't want to see him lost or hurt. Although the Forest
was generally filled with Fair Folk and good-natured
creatures, one could never be too careful. At least that
was Jory's opinion. After all, he hadn't ventured

beyond the clearing in longer than he could remember—perhaps since the last Great Gathering.

Word had spread throughout the Forest that the Council of Five had convened and another Great Gathering was upon them. Jory couldn't help but feel unusually adventurous about the whole thing. He was determined to have some fun. He had kissed the youngins good-bye and left them under the care and supervision of the yew tree. They had decided to stay behind, for the fear of not being able to eat with any regularity was too much for them. The Archer Spider declined as well, for he was concerned with much greater ideas like trying to get to the Moon! Jory had embarked with just a hint of uncertainty and a whole lot of anticipation. And so it was that Master Ra-Ma'at had gained a devoted travel companion. Of course, that was before the gnome's hunger set in.

They had found several traces of Taivyn's presence in the form of broken branches and a ripped piece of blue material hanging from one of the thorn bushes. Nothing really revealed anything beyond that, however. Taivyn had been through there, but as to what direction he might have continued on after that was completely unknown. By the time midday came, they were fatigued and decided to take a break for a bite to eat. Jory was gracious indeed. They knelt down beside a babbling brook whose waters ran sparkling and weaving around pebbles and river stones. The sun caught the flowing rivulets in various sections, making it look like a moving field of diamonds.

Master Ra-Ma'at broke out some brown bread, while Jory dug inside his pockets to reveal a stupendous stash of goods. How he fit all that into his pockets, Ra-Ma'at would never know. To the brown bread, Jory added some snapberries, a couple of red roots, and a few violets. The Master smiled at the assortment that lay before them.

After they had filled their bellies and replenished their spirits, they began to assess their surroundings. What happened next was anyone's good guess. Out from behind a bush trudged a rather large black bear. While years ago this might have given Master Ra-Ma'at great cause for concern, he now was remarkably calm. He stood up to greet the bear.

"Greetings to you, Great Chief of the Four-Legged Nation. To what do we owe the pleasure of this meeting?"

"Well," the bear began, "I have heeded the call in the air; I feel the invitation upon my breast, as you must, too. Once again, a Great Gathering is upon us. While, usually, we four-leggeds leave the affairs of Men and Faery to Men and Faery, a time is upon us that will affect us all. And so, it is with great curiosity that I am making my way to the Great Gathering place. I go as an onlooker only but with great interest indeed. I suppose that is where you two are going as well?"

"Er…well, yes, it is eventually. But first, I have something I must take care of beforehand if I am able. Seeing as we don't want to be late for the Great Gathering, I suppose we should be going."

The bear was always jovial, but one could never be too sure when his grumpy mood might set in, and so making interactions short and sweet was always helpful in avoiding confrontation. The bear didn't take a hint and offered, "Well, perhaps I could be of service in some way. Anything I might be able to help you with? I do owe you a favor, if you remember?"

Master Ra-Ma'at recalled the time when the bear had been in quite a dire situation. Both he and his little cub had been caught in a bear trap. It had been set by humans whose hearts and minds were already fast asleep, for they no longer remembered that divinity existed in all of life. The Master had stumbled upon the two bears during one of his Forest strolls, which used to happen with great frequency. He shuddered as a sad memory of his beloved Elysinia came into his mind—mostly why he didn't venture into the Forest as much these days; it just reminded him too much of her.

"Well, perhaps we could use your assistance. You haven't by any chance seen a young lad come through here. He is about yay big"—Ra-Ma'at held up his hand to indicate a height of nearly six feet tall and continued—"and he is basically alone and without a guide. He is quite young and a bit impetuous. He is inexperienced in the Forest, and he is in a great deal of danger if my suspicion is correct as to where he might be headed."

"Well, where do you feel he might be going?"

"I believe he is trying to find the location for the Crossing of the Frog and the Mushroom."

Something close to a gasp came out of the bear's jowl. "I see…" said the bear, not the least bit comforted. Then he continued, "Well, I must say there is only one that might know the timing and occurrence of that particular event, because I am told that she is mapping it quite seriously. The Record Keeper of the Faery Race—Elysinia."

"Really. Well, that is a good thing, because I am sure she will be at the Great Gathering. After we locate the boy, I plan to meet with my sister, Lunaya. Then, hopefully, together we can attend." Master Ra-Ma'at looked a bit confused for a moment.

He continued, "In fact, Brother Bear, would you do us a favor and point us in the direction of her dwelling place. I remember it being somewhere off the Polaris Ley Line, but I cannot seem to remember. And strangely enough, I have lost my sense of direction."

Master Ra-Ma'at looked around. He was sure that even though they had gotten off course to look for Taivyn, he could generally gage the direction by tuning into the various ley lines. He pulled out his map, and he was feeling quite dizzy. The bear understood at once what was happening.

He offered, "Sunny, if I may suggest, you step about thirty or so paces to the left, and I will be happy to explain the confusion you are feeling."

Ra-Ma'at did as the bear instructed. He began to feel much better. He looked around, and he suddenly felt reoriented to his surroundings. He was perplexed.

"Brother Bear, could you please tell me what just happened?"

"Yes, I believe you walked into a vortex. It has gotten stronger since last you were here. In fact, it may have just shown up altogether. We cannot really explain it; only that it demonstrates that the energies of the Earth Mother are indeed shifting now. We have these powerful spots springing up all over the place."

The Master was feeling much better. "This just confirms that there is not a moment longer to waste. Jory, we must redirect. We must reset our course, for the time is upon us and we cannot be late. I fear we are already working against the clock. And, furthermore, with the Crossing of the Frog and the Mushroom rapidly approaching, our timeline has drastically sped up."

Master Ra-Ma'at looked at Jory. The gnome nodded his agreement. Ra-Ma'at thanked the bear and started in the direction of Lunaya's tree cottage. He just hoped they weren't too late. He paused for just a second and looked up. As he did, he whispered a prayer for Taivyn.

"Great Father/Mother Creator, he is your child. Guide him, help him, comfort him. And please lead him to safety."

The Master closed his eyes and felt the Mother's energy coming up through the souls of his feet. He sent his love into her depths along with his prayer.

"Help him, Great Earth Mother. Nurture him. You are the only Mother the boy has."

He placed his hand in the side pocket of his robes and pulled out a little bundle. He unwrapped it to reveal some thyme and rosemary that he had gathered from the garden just days before setting off on this quest. He sprinkled it onto the ground and said, "Blessed Be."

Chapter 35
Kindred Spirits

*"Be Thou praised, oh Lord, for all Thy creation,
More especially for our Brother the Sun, who
bringeth forth the day,
Thou givest light thereby, for he is glorious and
splendid in his radiance to Thee..."*

—Saint Francis of Assisi, *"Hymn of the Sun"*

The Forest – 11,000 BCE

They followed the Polaris Ley Line. It ran almost parallel to the babbling brook they had sat down beside earlier for a bite to eat. Master Ra-Ma'at felt a rise in the sense of urgency in the air, and so his pace continued to increase steadily.

Jory struggled to keep up since his five steps equated to Master Ra-Ma'at's one. He sighed. It was okay. Jory was undoubtedly very excited to get out of the tree clearing. He was actually looking forward to the adventure. He knew the youngins would be well looked after. The tree would see to that. And they would be fed, which was most important. He wondered for just a moment if he had done the right thing by leaving them, but he quickly waived that feeling away with the rationalization that their most essential need (food) was being met.

They saw the willow tree ahead, which heralded Lunaya's tree cottage. The sun was taking his final steps of the day across the azure sky. Hopefully, they had arrived in time to catch his sister. He knew she would be leaving shortly if she hadn't already.

So here they were. Master Ra-Ma'at was almost nervous. He couldn't remember the last time he had seen Lunaya. They were twins, and since birth, they had shared a very special connection. He knew how dedicated she was to her work. He loved that about her; it inspired him. They had always been very devoted to one another and very supportive of each other's journey along the way. He was sad that she had decided to continue her studies deep within the Forest, but he knew it was for the best. She would best be able to master deeper levels of the Tree Mysteries in this way.

He and the tree gnome walked quietly over to the quaint little cottage. He didn't want to startle her, and yet, knowing Lunaya, her intuition would give them away instantly. When they came up to the door, he started to knock and the door opened. Lunaya's smile greeted them from the other side.

"Sunny! How wonderful to see you. I thought you'd never get here. Oh, my stars, I just can't believe my eyes. My dear brother! How I have missed you!"

They shared a warm embrace. There was no time to make small talk. "I would invite you in," said Lunaya, "but we have no time to spare. Am I correct in assuming that you came to accompany me to the Great Gathering?"

Lunaya then noticed Jory as she looked downward. "Jory! And to what do I owe this pleasure? I don't believe it. I didn't know that you were venturing outside of the tree these days! How are the children?"

Jory smiled a charming smile. He was clearly very proud of his youngins. His answer nearly surprised himself.

"Lady Lunaya, it is very good to see you. Yes, I must admit it has been ages! And yes, the children are wonderful, eating very well. Strong appetites those three. Yes, well, to answer your question: I am not exactly sure why I left. I guess it was time for me. You know, staying close to the home is good for gnomes; however, every now and then, it is important to stretch one's horizons and see what one can see…er…I mean…"

Lunaya looked just as surprised as the tree gnome. Then she looked at her brother and smiled. The three of them started laughing. When the laughter died down, Lunaya got serious. After all, she wanted to be supportive of the gnome's decision, "Well, that sounds just wonderful, dear. I am so happy to hear that. Tell me, will you be accompanying me to the Great Gathering?"

Not sure who the question was addressed to, both Ra-Ma'at and Jory responded in unison with a resounding, "Yes!"

"Well, wonderful. I must say, Jory, I never realized you had an interest in affairs such as these. Things really are changing."

Jory blushed, but somewhere deep down, he knew there was quite another reason he had left the safety of his tree clearing. That topic would have to be saved for later, because Lunaya continued on.

"Yes, well, there is something else that may need a little attention after the Great Gathering. I am not quite sure what course of action to take. It is rather a long story, but you see, we may have a visitor."

Chapter 36
An Eight-Legged Lesson

*"If we are to relearn the way of working with
the faeries...we must follow the ancient
pathways through the forest, where it is
sometimes dark, frightening, and perilous..."*

—Anna Franklin, *Working with Faeries*

The Forest – 11,000 BCE

Jedda awoke in a state of drowsiness. Her eyelids
were heavy, and she wasn't sure where she was. She
looked around and saw the trees and the birds and then
remembered what had happened. She rubbed her eyes,
as if that would help to clarify things. She glanced
around again. Well, she was not at her home on Brook
Lane anymore; that was obvious. She was also not in
that tree cottage, where she had landed after coming
through the tree last time. She wasn't quite sure where
she was. She wondered if she were even in the same
land she had been in before.

As she familiarized herself with her surroundings, she made some very interesting observations. At first glance, the Forest seemed normal enough, just like any other forest really. However, upon closer inspection, something was positively different.

She began to slowly recall the events that had led up to her decision to enter the tree. She remembered the faery lights like glowing orbs dancing to and fro. They were enchanting. It was more stunning than the most marvelous light show. Couple that up with a strong otherworldly overtone, and it still didn't even come close to summing up the experience. Too bad. Jedda liked things that she could sum up.

And so, it was in the midst of this spellbinding and indescribable experience with the faery lights that Jedda had decisively proceeded, or rather thoughtlessly advanced once again, into the willow tree. She shook her head. Everyday seemed to add a new dimension to her life, literally. She did have to wonder if she was just imagining it all. If this didn't pan out, she might seriously have to consider a therapist.

She remembered her refreshing conversation with Lou then. Even though the facts were hard to swallow with her rational mind, her heart knew that everything was pure truth. Imagine a moment when all the things that one believed in when he or she was a child are confirmed once and for all. Then, suddenly, the world just feels a little lighter, a little more joyful, and somewhere you know that magic exists.

As Jedda considered her surroundings, she noticed that the colors of this place were a thousand times more vivid than she remembered them being in other forests, or in life as a whole for that matter. It was as if she had been wearing tinted shades all her life, and the shades were suddenly removed to reveal a radiant world before her. She took a few more steps. Then she started to notice a peculiar sensation rise up from the bottoms of her feet. The Earth was pulsating. This was strange indeed.

Everything started to look oddly familiar, like she had been here once before. Could it be? The Forest in her dreams. She walked up to one of the giant trees that stood before her. There was an audible tune, like a humming sound, coming from it. The sound was reminiscent of a wind chime blowing in the breeze. It seemed like it was coming from up high in the tree. She looked up. At first, she didn't see anything.

Then, upon further investigation, she realized she was staring straight at the sound or rather what was making the sound. It was a rather large spider. She stood there in shock. She didn't think she had ever seen a bug as large as this—not even on those animal shows. This spider was an immense anomaly, as far as Jedda was concerned. It was so large that it was disturbing. Repulsed, she started to retreat when to her surprise, she was jolted into stopping.

"Well, excuse me, Miss, but you don't look so great yourself. You humans are so interesting the way you shy away from bugs, as you like to call us. Without us, and I do mean spiders in particular, you wouldn't have your beloved stories. After all, we taught humans how to weave a tale. Through our very existence, we also hold the light for the idea of the interconnectedness of Life. Without us, that memory may very well fade away. And let me tell you. You humans really need all the help you can get."

Jedda felt slightly ashamed, although still aghast. She tried to atone for her hasty and rather discourteous reaction.

"My apologies, but I am not accustomed to bugs your size. Pardon my impolite reaction. I was just quite taken aback, and I must admit that I still am."

Jedda looked up to see if her justification had sufficed. She had become quite good at making up excuses in Mr. Ramen's class. Seemingly satisfied with her explanation, the spider continued, "Well, I do suppose I can understand that. Do tell me just where is it that you come from that you do not have creatures of my size. You look to be about my size...hmmm."

"Ah yes, I didn't say we did not have creatures of your size, for in fact we do. We have lots of animals your size, and some even quite a bit bigger. And, of course, humans are my size, well, the smaller ones! But I meant insects. Insects. We don't have insects your size. And, to answer your question, I am from Maine in the United States on Earth."

Just then the spider began to laugh uproariously. He laughed so hard he nearly fell out of the tree. Jedda, not seeing what was so humorous, became a little annoyed. The spider quickly picked up on her mood and decided not to keep her in the dark any longer.

"Well, first of all, just to clarify—I am NOT an insect. I don't know what they teach humans where you are from, but insects have six legs. See count. One, Two, Three, Four…"

Jedda interrupted as she could see where this was going. "Yes, yes, of course. I realize you are a spider. I know spiders have eight legs and are not technically insects. They are from the arachnid family. Yes. I know. I am sorry. So that is what you found so terribly funny?"

"Well, no, of course not; I found that to be terribly insulting. However, the comment you made after that made me overlook the insult and become hysterical. You said you lived on the planet Ear…" Before the spider could get the whole word out, he dropped to the ground and began rolling around and cackling uncontrollably.

"Well, what's so funny about that?" Jedda snapped. For goodness' sake, why did the spider find this so hilarious? He acted as if this world were just completely normal. Well, Jedda supposed it was perhaps normal—for him!

The spider finally calmed down long enough to speak, "All right, all right. I am sorry. It's just that. Well, of course, we are on Earth. I mean can't you feel her?" The spider continued, "The Earth has a very specific vibration like an energy signature of sorts."

Jedda looked perplexed, "Energy signature, huh? I really have no idea what you are talking about. And, if you don't mind, I really don't want to waste any more time. I simply must be going!"

The spider got serious then. "Listen. I'm sorry. Let's start over, shall we? They call me the Archer

Spider. You can just call me Spider if you like. Would you like to tell me who you are?"

"Yes, sure, I guess so." Jedda was obviously frustrated. "My name is Jedda. And while we are on this introduction bit, I might add that no, I wasn't sure if this was still considered Earth. Quite frankly, I'm not sure if I am in a dream or if this is real. The fact that there are giant spiders, though, is sure making me lean toward the former. All I remember is that one moment I was at home in Maine. The next, I was seeing faery lights in the tree. Next, I saw that vesica piscis symbol again. Then, I don't know, perhaps the moon spoke to me. That part I'm not so sure about. One minute, I was standing there, asking some Higher Power for some answers. The next minute, this door opened in the tree—my favorite tree, by the way, the willow tree in front of my house. I wasn't sure if it opened in answer to my prayer or if it was the moon communicating with me, or if perhaps maybe God does exist. I was not sure. All I know is that it opened, just as it had before, and then I went in. And here I am."

The spider's whole demeanor changed. Up until now, he had been playful and lighthearted. Suddenly, he got very serious and said, "Are you saying that you came through a tree portal?"

Jedda thought about his question for a moment and then responded, "Yes, I suppose you could say that. I am not quite sure what happened. Like last time, a door appeared and I just walked through it. The only thing is that, last time, I ended up in a different place when I came through to the other side."

The spider was thoughtful for a moment. "The thing with tree portals is…and I don't know much because that is definitely not my area of expertise, as I mentioned earlier. The thing with tree portals is that they follow your intentions. They always take you on a journey according to what is within you. You connect and work with them through your heart. They respond to your true heart's desires."

"What if I didn't have a desire or wish at the time? What if I had no sense of direction whatsoever? What if I am lost because I was a girl who was lost in that moment when I entered that doorway?"

"You always have something deep within your heart. Even if you are not consciously aware of it, it is there. Believe me. That's what half the stories I tell are about. Think about how you were feeling at the time you went through or just before."

Jedda reflected back on that moment. Everything had happened so quickly she was not sure what her intentions had been. She thought about how she had been feeling. Then she realized it!

"Oh my God! I know now! I know. Well, I don't exactly know, but I do sort of know. At least I know what I was feeling at the time. At the moment when I chose to go into the tree, I was feeling a mixture of emotions: sadness, despair, enchantment. Most of all, though, I had just made a plea to God, or the universe, or whoever was listening. I wanted to understand. I didn't want to feel alone any longer. I wanted to know what was going on and who I was. I remembered what the raven had said to me before we parted ways. He

211

said that soon I would have to make a choice. And the decision was all mine. However, he said that I would have to choose if I wished to know. Actually, he used the word 'remember'—if I wished to remember. He said I would have to choose to remember and awaken to my purpose or not. If I chose to remember, I would have to reconnect with my past if I wished to embrace my purpose in the present. He said it was up to me, however."

Jedda was pensive. She became deep in thought, pondering the magnitude of her choice. She wondered at the possibility that she might have actually begun the journey of doing just that: remembering.

The Archer Spider was amazed. "I am speechless, which does not happen often as I have an excellent command of all language, you see. But your story, while I admit it could have used a little finesse, which I am sure you will work out next time you tell it, was captivating."

The spider thought about all she had said and what it could all mean, and then he continued, "Lady Jedda, if I may call you by that name, I must say that I do not know what all of this means. I do know that if indeed you used a tree portal, which it sounds like you have, then that is very interesting indeed, because there are very few who have the ability to use the tree portals, most of which are members of the Faery Race! There are a few who have been taught to do so, but clearly, that is not what you have explained to me here. In fact, it sounds like you had no idea what you were doing."

Jedda was still not sure she understood what the Archer Spider was trying to convey here. Clearly, she was not a faery. Did she look like she had wings? She turned around and looked over her shoulder just to be sure. If this was a dream, anything was possible. Nope, no wings there. She breathed a concealed sigh of relief.

"Did you say you might have talked to the moon?" The spider grew very quiet now.

"Yes?" Jedda answered, wondering where this was going.

"What did she say?" The spider's question was filled with childlike innocence.

"I'm not sure exactly, but I felt like she said that the answers I am seeking are found within," Jedda answered, not quite sure what the spider was looking for.

"Ah," the spider sighed, "somehow I always knew that was what she'd say." He had a dreamy, faraway look in his eyes. Then, as quickly as he had drifted away, he was back with full attention.

"There is another bit of your tale that is of interest to me. You mentioned a raven. Did this raven have a name?"

Jedda tried to remember the bird's name. It was rather unusual. Then it came to her. "Yes, the raven's name was Yuri."

The Archer Spider brought two of his eight legs up to the place on his head that could be perceived as a chin and scratched; he was deep in thought. "Ah, I see…"

Jedda looked up very interested in what the Spider might have to say. He appeared to be holding back for some reason. Then he continued, "Well, Yuri is known in these parts. He has, as of late, been working diligently at something with the Lady Lunaya; however, ultimately, he is a bird in service to the Faery Race."

Jedda really had no idea what the spider was talking about at this point; she was completely lost. All this talk about Faeries. She decided, while she had someone here willing to offer her the answers she sought—at least those he knew, she might as well take advantage of the opportunity.

"So, just to clarify, you keep mentioning the Faery Race. I assume you mean the faeries like the ones I saw glowing in the trees. The little sparkling globes of light?"

"Not exactly." The spider was thoughtful for a moment, trying to decide the best way to explain, for much of this was just commonplace for him, and he was not really sure how he knew of it or understood it.

He attempted an explanation. "I suppose you could say that those light beings you are referring to are part of the Faerie Kingdom; however, it is not to those that I refer. You see, those small faeries are indeed very important in the Divine Plan, for their role upon this green Earth is to support the individual growth process of something living. They usually have jobs like helping flowers grow or seeing to it that a particular crystal being realizes its fullest potential.

"However, the Faery Beings whom I refer to are no more important, but much more greatly evolved. They are essentially what many of us call the Ancient Ones, for they are said to have come from the stars. Those Faery Beings to whom I refer, why their job is to see to it that the Earth, herself, reaches her fullest potential as a divinely guided being in the Great Divine Plan. They are essentially midwives who support her in her evolutionary path forward. They are the ones who know about the trees. They are those who know and speak the first seed language, Elyrie—the Language of the Trees."

Jedda thought back to all her mother's picture books and faery stories. She supposed that she remembered all different types of Faery beings, big and small. She thought about gnomes, sprites, and pixies. Of course, whoever truly knew what the difference was between all those different faeries? It had never really occurred to her.

So now, here she was, talking to a spider, and this great understanding was coming to her. Amazing! Simply amazing! She was a little mystified by all this talk of a Divine Plan and the Creator, especially hearing it from a spider. Strange. But the world works in mysterious ways, she thought to herself. And whoever made up that quote, well give that person a cookie! They hit the nail on the nose with that one.

"Well, Spider, I want to thank you for all your time. I believe we may have gotten off to a rocky start, but I feel like things have improved considerably. And so we part as friends?"

"Why, yes, of course, we part as friends. I hope you find the answers you are seeking. For only you can really know when you find what you are searching for. If I may ever again be of any service, please feel free to stop by this clearing. You can know it by the particular trees that create an enclosure here." The spider indicated the group of yews that formed a sort of crescent moon shape around the space.

Jedda was very grateful that her first encounter with a being from this land had been a friendly one. She hoped there were not any creatures that she had to look out for. She thought about asking the spider but then decided against it. She did not need anything more to worry about.

She hesitated still. Some question inside of her was still lurking. She wondered what that question might be. Something was trying to present itself. She wanted to ask something else, but she couldn't figure out what it was. It was on the tip of her tongue. Then it came to her. She knew that the logical thing to do was to ask the spider about the whereabouts of Yuri, but what came out instead was: "Spider, one last thing...would you be so kind as to tell me where I could find the Faeries you speak of?"

Jedda did not know why that came out of her mouth, but it had. She had no idea what she would even do or say if or when she found them, but some still small voice from deep within her surfaced to say, "It is with the Faeries that you will find your answers."

She didn't even know the questions, let alone the answers. She only knew that she had begun this journey, and she could not turn back. Not now, not ever. Jedda Rose Delaney was sure of herself. She knew she was on the right path. There was nothing else. The thought of finding the Faeries evoked a longing within her soul. She had always believed them to be real when she was a little girl, but this went beyond that. It was as if some distant song were calling her home. Home to what? She looked at the spider longingly. He recognized that emotion well, because he himself often felt it; he was sure he looked the same. He knew that was how he felt when he looked to the Moon, where the Grandmother dwelt.

"I know of many places they can be found. For there are many dwelling places of the Fair Folk in this Forest. There are many entrances to their realm hidden within Faery Mounds or underneath a Faery Ring. They are everywhere and nowhere. The thing is they can only be found if they want to be found. That is the challenge that you face. However, I suppose they may present themselves to you if indeed your intentions are pure."

The Archer Spider paused there in order to receive some sort of agreement from the young and determined girl. After all, he couldn't be the cause of giving away secret information regarding their whereabouts if she meant them harm or other injury. He had to be certain, and he had to have a verbal promise.

Jedda shook her head, agreeing very rapidly, so as not to dissuade him from sharing what he knew. She followed this motion up by quickly affirming out loud, "Yes, my intentions are pure."

After she spoke those words, she thought about what that meant exactly and clarified, perhaps to the spider, perhaps to herself. "My intentions are pure in that I do not wish to do any harm. However, I do seek answers for myself. I have a sense that somehow they can help me understand what is happening, and somehow they can help me…remember." Jedda used the word awkwardly since it was not her own; it was the one the bird used when referring to her situation.

For the spider, that was sufficient. He said, "Well, okay then. I think that should be good enough. So, as I mentioned, there are a great many places where you can gain entrance to their realm, but you would not see them if you did not know or were not invited. Therefore, I will tell you somewhere you may go where you are sure to find them, if they are indeed there. It is a very sacred place; some say the oak trees within this place are the most ancient on all the Earth. You will know it by the perfect circle that they form. Within this perfect circle stands one tree, great and mighty. This one is often referred to as the Old One or the Great Oak. It is here that you may find what you seek, for it is here that the Faeries often abide."

Jedda's eyes became wide with awe. She exclaimed, "Why that sounds just like the place in my dream! I cannot believe it. This is incredible. How do I get there?"

"That is a good question indeed. And I do not have the answer to tell you. I could tell you to go this way or that, but really, you must follow your heart. For then and only then will you arrive at this place. This place is a microcosm for the Forest in general. It exists on many different levels. Some may see it, some may not. Some may seek it, but may never find it. I can only tell you that you must set your intention in a loving and good way and listen to your heart. Your heart will guide you to this place. This place is really a part of all of us."

Jedda understood in some very profound way. She knew that what the spider had spoken was true. She considered for a moment before asking her next question. Then she said, "How do I begin?"

"Like this…" And the Archer Spider began the hypnotic melody he had been humming when she had first arrived in the Forest. The sound of wind chimes filled the air again. Then, suddenly, she noticed that the sound filled her. It reverberated within her cells, creating an inner dance of light. And so, by the spider's song, she was led into the depths of her heart and soul.

Chapter 37
The Moon and the Sun

*"The greatest delight the fields and woods
minister is the suggestion of an occult relation
between man and the vegetable. I am not
alone and unacknowledged. They nod to me
and I to them."*

—Ralph Waldo Emerson

Willow Tree Cottage – 11,000 BCE

"A visitor?" Master Ra-Ma'at peered around Lunaya inside her tree cottage. Lunaya chuckled. She had missed her brother so much.

"Not in there, silly. I've forgotten how even in the most serious of times you always manage to make me laugh. Ah, Sunny, I love you!"

Ra-Ma'at was not so sure he understood what she meant, or what was so funny. Lunaya understood his bewilderment.

"What I meant was that I believe someone may have used a tree portal to come here from another time and place. You see, I've been working with the Faeries and Yuri, the raven, on something big. I think it might have to do with that. Anyway, I will tell you all about it along the way."

By this time, Jory was playing with a patch of grass. Apparently, a tree gnome's attention span was slightly longer than that of a goldfish. Ra-Ma'at, however, was very interested.

"Does this have something to do with the darkness and trepidation that I have been feeling? I know that the feelings are related to the impending Dark Cycle that is upon us; I'm just not exactly sure how or why."

"More than likely, yes. I don't know how all the pieces fit together, but I am starting to see a bigger picture at play than I could have ever imagined…" Lunaya was pondering something.

"I will tell you everything I know on the way. We cannot linger here much longer if we intend to make the Great Gathering by midnight. So, are you prepared to start the journey then?" She was finished for the time being, but they obviously had much to discuss.

Master Ra-Ma'at indicated, "I'm as ready as I'll ever be!" Lunaya sensed there was something in his voice that really meant it.

"We must make haste then!"

And with that they made ready to leave.

They grabbed a few extra provisions, and then together the three of them departed. They were leaving just as the sun was setting. Hopefully, they would not arrive too late to the Great Gathering place. The journey would take several hours, and that was if they didn't stop or get slowed down for any reason.

They swiftly walked on without a second thought. All but Jory of course. Jory looked back longingly. He thought to himself about food and rubbed his belly. Oh, well, for the first time in his whole life, Jory would have to wait to eat.

Ra-Ma'at and Lunaya, however, were just thrilled about their upcoming adventure. To be making the trip together was such a blessing. It would give them some much-needed time to catch up. First, Lunaya wanted to finish explaining the story she had begun earlier.

"Ultimately, I have attuned to the Forest enough that I can detect that a tree portal has been used. Someone new has definitely arrived here just recently. I can feel it."

Ra-Ma'at was pleased to see Lunaya's progress. He knew the Faeries had initiated her deep into the Mysteries of the Trees; the profound effect of these studies, however, had not been apparent until now. His sister's dedication and adeptness never ceased to amaze him. That she was able to feel the nuances within the Forest with such preciseness to know that a visitor had arrived through a tree portal was just short of miraculous. It was absolutely brilliant. He was proud of his sister.

"Well, is this a cause for concern? Could it be one who wished us or this land harm?" Ra-Ma'at asked, not concealing his alarm.

"I don't think so," Lunaya reassured him. "It doesn't feel like that's the case. I am actually not sure what the purpose of this one coming to our land is, nor am I sure of their exact identity."

"How do you know they do not wish harm?" Master Ra-Ma'at wasn't convinced.

"I know because, in studying the Tree Mysteries, I have learned that a person with malicious intentions cannot work with tree portals. They wouldn't be able to come through. One must be pure of heart. You can manipulate many things in nature, but you cannot manipulate the trees, or the Faeries who work with them."

The Master was slightly more satisfied with her answer this time around, but he still had questions, "So, where are they?"

"Well, they could be anywhere..." Lunaya was suddenly interrupted by Jory clearing his throat. "Yes, Jory, did you want to add something?"

"Well, of course, I would like to add something. You see, trees are my area of expertise. Of course, I don't work with them like the Shining Ones do, but I am a tree gnome. Hmmphh!" Jory snorted his obvious annoyance at being excluded from the discussion. After he felt like he had made his point, and that he had their full attention, he added, "Yes, well, all I wanted to say is that if one were pure in heart, and used a tree portal, then that person would go to the obvious place—a place that their heart desired. Which, according to what you all are saying, happened to be this Forest for some reason yet unknown to us all."

"Oh my! It's her!" Lunaya gasped. "It must be. No one else would know about this place and time and fit these criteria, and I expect that *bird* to be with her."

Lunaya said the word "bird" with a particular emphasis that could only indicate her agitation with the winged one.

"It's who?" Ra-Ma'at and Jory were both confused.

"Jedda. Her name is Jedda," Lunaya confirmed. She decided this might be a good time to recount the story to her brother, at least the parts she knew.

"It all started when I sent the raven, Yuri, on a mission. Basically, the mission was to locate a Keeper of the Moon Clan in a future time—a time that sits across from us on the Astrological Wheel of the Ages. The details aren't really important now; however, what he found is extremely significant somehow. What he found was a complete anomaly."

Lunaya quickly recounted the abbreviated version of Yuri's tale, including the part about the mystery of the young girl named Jedda. Ra-Ma'at was following as much as he could, given the plethora of information with which his sister was bombarding him. Lunaya gave him another minute to process everything.

Then she continued, "When Yuri reported what he had found to Elysinia, she seemed satisfied. I am not sure why, because we still had not located one of the future Keepers. Additionally, Elysinia urged Yuri to return, not to find a current Keeper but to connect with this young girl again."

"Well, what does this mean?" her brother wondered.

"It doesn't mean anything. It can't. We don't have time for it, too. Whatever it means, we'll have to wait until after the Great Gathering. We must press on regardless."

Master Ra-Ma'at and Lunaya altered their pace to a gait. They wished to reach the two boulders before midnight, for that signaled the entranceway of the Great Gathering. Jory had complained at least a dozen times about his withering stomach. He was sure he was being led to certain death—an unnecessary, self-imposed famine, he called it.

Lunaya and Ra-Ma'at just smiled. They were happy to be back within each other's company. It had been such a long time. Why they had waited so long to reconnect was incomprehensible. They decided to shift the conversation to something light. Lunaya asked to be caught up on all the happenings of the community. Ra-Ma'at talked about the last Festival of Lights. He spoke of some of the elders, whom Lunaya did see from time to time when they traveled deep in the Forest. He talked about Korin and all the young pupils in training. Then he felt a pang of guilt grip him. Lunaya sensed the sudden shift in his demeanor. He couldn't hide anything from her.

"What's wrong?" she asked. "Why the sudden forlorn face? Come on, Sunny. Talk to me. What happened?"

"I had hoped to arrive earlier to the Great Gathering; I wanted some extra time before it started to visit the Crystal Library. There is a prophecy in that collection. I feel that it may be another piece to all of this."

Master Ra-Ma'at was obviously still tormented about Taivyn leaving. He swallowed hard, feeling a little ashamed that he had been so wrapped up in his mission that he had failed to see a young one in need. He finally confessed.

"Lunaya, I've failed. Because of my lack of attention, something terrible has occurred. I believe that I am partly to blame for it." Ra-Ma'at sighed and went on, "Do you remember the young boy Taivyn?"

"Well, of course, I remember the boy Taivyn! You were very fond of him. You said he reminded you of yourself when you were a boy."

"Yes, well, he has run away!" There, the cat was out of the bag.

"What! Why that's terrible? When did it happen? Where has he gone?"

Ra-Ma'at recounted the story. He told her about how the boy had followed him into the Forest. He also confessed that he had originally instructed the boy to return to the community by morning. Then he told her how he'd had a change of heart, but it was too late, because Taivyn had fled in the middle of the night.

"Where do you think he went?"

"That's the other thing. He overheard me speaking to Korin of the prophecy and how it may pertain to him. The problem is that he has no idea which prophecy I was talking about. Later, when he heard us discourse about the frog and the mushroom, he assumed it was the prophecy to which I had referred!"

"What! Well, he can't mean to wield the power of their crossing. I mean he isn't ready for something such as that. He wouldn't know what to do with it. He could also ruin a very rare and unique opportunity." Lunaya was very worried.

"Yes, which is why we searched for him this morning, but it was no use. He was gone without hardly a trace. I don't know where he went, and I haven't heard anything from any of the forest animals or Fair Folk."

"Neither have I. Elysinia will know what to do. She has been watching this event very closely. I don't know all the details yet, but she plans to crystal record the conjunction. I believe we will be given full disclosure at the Great Gathering."

Lunaya was a little flustered but continued, "It has something to do with preserving the sacred teachings. Like a safety mechanism beyond that of the Keepers."

"Interesting…" Ra-Ma'at trailed off. He was deep in thought. "I wonder what she plans to do with that energy…."

Chapter 38
Stars and Soul Mates

"Out beyond ideas of wrongdoing
and rightdoing there is a field.
I'll meet you there.
When the soul lies down in that grass
The world is too full to talk about."

—Rumi

The Forest – 11,000 BCE

J edda continued moving through the Forest. She had no rational sense of direction. When she made a choice to turn or move straight ahead, it wasn't based on any form of reason; she was simply following her heart. She could still hear the spider's song within her. She wondered if every creature had a song they called their own. How beautiful life must be if that were the case!

She didn't know how long she went on like this—it could have been minutes or years—for it wouldn't have mattered either way. Then, suddenly, the song her heart was singing became her own. It was in that moment that a glorious vision appeared before her eyes. As if out of nowhere, a perfectly formed circle of trees materialized just up ahead.

She instantly quickened her pace; so focused was she on what laid in front of her. She became so exuberant that she even began to skip wildly. Without any inhibitions, she was hopping and frolicking swiftly and with delight. Then suddenly—CRASH!

She slammed into something so hard that the wind was knocked right out of her lungs. She didn't know what had hit her. Lying on her back, she really thought she might be seeing stars. She tried to peel herself off the ground when she heard a worried voice.

"Oh, My Lady! I am so sorry. Please forgive my foolishness. I wasn't looking where I was going! I am so sorry. Here, My Lady, let me help you up."

Still dizzy, she took the hand of the one who spoke. As she did, she experienced the sensation of warm lightning moving down her arm and throughout her whole body. She allowed herself to be pulled up gently. Then she looked into the eyes of the one who held her steady.

A young man with dreamy green eyes met her gaze. She was speechless, breathless, and not just from the fall. He had pleasantly warm sandy brown hair, and his cheeks had a slightly rosy hue to them. He was a bit unkempt, and there seemed to be quite a bit of leaves and dirt on his clothing. Jedda couldn't be sure if it was from the collision, or from a collection that had built up over a period of time. When they spoke again, it was at the same time, and so they both apologized, not wanting to appear ill-mannered. Jedda suddenly felt a little shy. She silently chided herself for being so overcome by this young man. Finally, it was he who spoke again.

"My Lady, allow me to introduce myself. My name is Taivyn Green, and I am on a quest. I am, however, at your service for the time being, seeing as though I practically ran you over. Again, my sincerest apologies."

Taivyn didn't know what had come over him. The last time he was this polite was at that dance the Moon Clan community put on several years ago. He didn't even want to attend, let alone have to be polite then. He was just sort of forced into it. Here, he couldn't think of any other way to talk to this beautiful girl before him. He lost himself in her eyes, which were a sparkling blue not unlike the beautiful lake where he used to take the horses for a drink while living at the community. She was very small, and she looked to be about his age.

In fact, what was a young girl of his age doing, wandering about alone like this in the Forest anyway? For some reason, he felt immediately protective of her. He did not understand how or why he was feeling the way he did in that moment, but it was unlike anything else he had ever experienced. Something about this girl was different, very different.

Jedda thought she better say something before this handsome boy thought she was a mute. "I'm fine, really. Apology accepted. It is possible that it could have been a little my fault, too," Jedda scowled. She hated admitting she might be in the wrong.

Taivyn interjected at once, "Never, My Lady. I wouldn't hear of it. I am sure you were not at fault, nor could you ever be for anything."

Jedda smiled. She definitely liked the sound of that. She continued, "Well, thank you, Taivyn. My name is Jedda. I am on a sort of quest myself. In fact, I believe I may have reached my destination. That is why I was skipping so rapidly, because I was really excited." Jedda signaled the clearing just ahead with the perfectly formed circle of oak trees.

Taivyn gazed at the clearing to which Jedda referred. Then he looked back at her and held her gaze for moments or an eternity. He couldn't be sure. He felt all sorts of conflicting emotions rise up. On one hand, he felt completely and utterly mesmerized by this young girl who appeared out of nowhere and claimed to be on a quest. If that were the case, she was a girl after his own heart. On the other, how could this young girl be on a quest of her own? Did girls even go on quests? He supposed they did. There was the Lady Lunaya who went off on a type of quest. Lady Astriel, too, would go off into the Forest from time to time. Now that he thought about it, yes, indeed, women went on quests, but did young girls? He felt his protective instinct that he didn't even know he had bubble up again.

Suddenly, nothing mattered any longer. He just wanted to keep her safe. He instantly forgot about his own personal quest. Who needed to find some frog and mushroom anyway? Besides, what would he do if he were to find them? Then what? No, that was it. He didn't know what had come over him. He felt as if the stars and the moon had aligned somewhere between his heart and soul. This feeling was unexplainable.

Now, it was not to say that Taivyn wasn't well-versed with the ladies in general. Many of the young girls seemed to like the idea that the circumstances surrounding his origin were ambiguous at best. They thought it was mysterious. Yes, he thought about all the girls and their crushes.

This was definitely nothing like that. This was entirely unique. Something magical and timeless pervaded this moment, and the feeling deepened each time they looked at one another. Somehow, Taivyn knew that he never wanted to let her go.

"Well, Lady Jedda, if I may accompany you to your final destination. I should like to see that you stay out of harm's way. Would you oblige me and allow me to escort you there? I promise not to get in the way. I do understand the importance of a great quest."

Taivyn offered this and hoped like hell that she would agree. In all actuality, he couldn't fathom the thought of ever not accompanying her or being by her side. For now, this would have to do, though.

Jedda was glad for the company. She certainly could use it. She really hadn't seen or spoken to anyone since the Archer Spider, and that wasn't even a human. No, she would definitely welcome the companionship. Of course, she knew in her heart of hearts that there was definitely more to it than that. She looked into his eyes once again. It was as if she had known him all her life, and yet they had just met. She couldn't explain this uncanny connection between them. Then she remembered. "But, Taivyn, what about your quest?"

"My Lady Jedda, I have waited sixteen years for answers that I hope my quest will illuminate. However, I have no doubt that these answers will wait for me a while longer as I escort you to your journey's end. In fact, no quest could be more important than making certain that you arrive safely to your destination. Allow me to have this honor."

He offered his hand. Jedda took it without thought. Again, she felt electricity move like little shock waves throughout her whole being. Her heart was racing. She could feel a fire burning within. She looked over at him and wondered if he felt it, too. Judging by the look of sheer pleasure on his face, she was certain he did.

They walked hand in hand. The sun had just set in the distance just above the trees. The sky was left with swirling lavenders and pinks that seemed like a reflection of what these two felt in their souls. For that is how one feels when they meet their twin flame, regardless of the distance or time between them; they are as one.

They arrived at the edge of the clearing in sheer bliss. Jedda looked at Taivyn and then back at the trees. Something was so familiar, like a distant memory that resided on some high cliff within the expansiveness of her being. It rested there beyond time and space, as if waiting to be set free. It flickered within her like a burning candle flame that she never wanted to blow out—ever again. She let his hand go, and he understood.

Chapter 39
I Know You

"The earth has disappeared beneath my feet,
It fled from all my ecstasy,

Now like a singing air creature
I feel the Rose
Keep opening."

—Hafiz

The Forest – 11,000 BCE

They were so connected he knew her mind. He knew that she did not intend to leave him just yet. She only meant to approach the circle of trees by herself, for there was something there for her that she had to experience alone.

She looked at him one last time before making this journey that was both short and long. He smiled, assuring her that he would wait for her there. Jedda moved toward the circle with poise and calm. She was so entranced in the present moment that she did not recognize how like her dream this moment really was. She could hear the stories of the Forest all around her. She even thought she heard the song of a frog and a mushroom. How she identified that sound, she did not know. She could hear a babbling brook in the distance, and the wind whispering to the trees of where it had been.

Then she entered the circle. She loved these trees, and she knew they loved her as well. She moved ever so slowly to the innermost part of the circle. She saw the Great Oak, or the Old One, as she knew him to be called. She looked up and saw Yuri sitting on his highest branch, watching her intently to see what she would do next.

As she approached the Great Oak, a radiant light grew within her heart. This luminescence grew brighter and brighter. She got up close to this beautiful Standing One. She brought her delicate hands up and placed them reverently upon his trunk. She breathed softly. The bark felt warm beneath her touch. Like small rivers of light, the sap was moving up and down the tree. Jedda could feel the tree's life-force energy pulsing into her palms. She felt the energy move into her like a river of love that opened her up to infinity. Time stood still. She could see the rings within the tree somehow. Like a vision, they appeared in her mind's eye.

Then she heard the Language of the Trees. The Tree spoke to her of many things. It spoke to her of life, death, and rebirth. It spoke to her about time—past, present, and future. It shared with her many secrets of the universe. Like a great universal library, these records were opened unto her. Some call these the

Akashic Records; to Jedda, these were the Records of Time stored within the rings of the tree.

She saw the symbol that had been the catalyst for her journey's commencement. The beginning? That felt like so long ago. The vesica piscis floated within her, or was it within the tree? She wasn't sure.

She sent love to the tree, grateful for its wisdom and light. She honored it for all that it was. She slowly allowed her hands to fall away. She turned to press her back up against its trunk, for it was strength that she needed now. She thanked it for all it had shared with her. As she turned to walk away, Jedda noticed a gossamer form standing just barely within the circle of trees.

This One she saw had auburn hair infused with golden light that looked hewn by the sun's very own rays. Her skin was shimmering white and appeared to reflect the stars. This One walked or floated over to where Jedda stood; it was hard to tell. Upon her head, she wore a silver ring with a symbol etched upon it at the brow point. The vesica piscis. This One moved, but didn't move. She walked, but didn't walk. Even though they had not yet spoken, Jedda knew this being was of the Faery Race.

"Welcome, Dear One. I am glad you are here. I have waited for you. I knew you would come. We are of a different time—you and I—and yet we are not. In your time, the Faery Ones exist, but not as we once did. For time has changed, and the light upon the Earth is different now. In your time, the Earth is preparing for her Great Awakening. In this time, we are helping her to prepare for sleep. She will go into a sort of hibernation—along with most of mankind. My people exist somewhat outside of time and space now. However, it wasn't always this way. Don't you remember…Rose?"

Jedda was shocked. How did this one know her middle name? "Rose is my second name. I don't understand how you know that. Only my family ever uses that name. And I don't understand why this place feels so familiar. It's as if I've been here before. But I have not."

The Shining One, as they were called, spoke suddenly, "Ah, but you have. Perhaps not as you are now. Not as your human self. But you have indeed been here. This place is a part of you. It is a part of your heart. Remember."

With those words, the Faery Woman placed her fingers upon Jedda's brow. A great sparkling light emanated forth. Then the Faery touched Jedda's heart and activated something deep and seemingly forgotten.

Something stirred within Jedda. The memory that had been lingering somewhere in the forgotten lands of her consciousness suddenly rose to the surface. The young girl saw in a flash the fragmented memory made whole. Jedda remembered. She remembered who she was and what her choice had been so long ago. She remembered. She started to speak, but the beautiful one held her hand to her lips. This was not to be expressed in words.

"You are to keep this memory sacred for now. This is just the beginning. You have begun to remember. In this time, this still has not yet occurred, and so we must not speak it aloud in this place, for it could alter the very threads of time and space. You must go now. Go back to your land. You have much to do there."

"But I don't want to leave. Please I have finally found home. And…" Jedda peered through the circle of trees, at the one who had been waiting for her. She blushed when she saw him there and felt a warm sensation in her heart.

The Shining One understood. "Listen to me. This cannot be. I know you cannot understand this now, but know that this cannot be now. You must return to your time and your land. Eventually, you will come to understand. You each have a very important destiny to fulfill, and you cannot fulfill it here together. Therefore, you cannot stay. It was difficult enough to bring you here and gift you with this experience, this understanding, but it cannot be more than that. I am sorry."

A tear slid down Jedda's face. She didn't know what had come over her. How could she feel so torn and broken at the thought of leaving this young man whom she had hardly even known? It didn't make any rational sense, and she didn't care to understand either.

"What shall I do…? I'm sorry I didn't get your name."

"Elysinia. My name is Elysinia. I am the Record Keeper of the Faery Race. I hold the crystals of time so that wisdom is never lost, only misplaced or forgotten. And I am the fifth element in the Council of Five. This is why the vesica piscis brought you to me. For it is a symbol that contains within it the perfect balance of both the Divine Masculine and the Divine Feminine. It is about the integration of both these energies that breeds perfect harmony. It is the fifth element that unites all others. It is Divine Love."

"Elysinia…" Jedda repeated the name as if she had heard it once before once upon time, once in a dream. She looked back at Taivyn. "What do I say to him?"

"You do not. It is time to go for now. You can return at another time, but now the time is not."

Jedda started crying. She felt such a deep and unexplainable sense of loss and sadness right now. She didn't know how she was going to go on. It was like she had found home, and now it was being ripped out from under her. As excruciating as the pain was, she knew that the words that Elysinia spoke were truth. She knew she could not remain, and yet she could not bear the thought of leaving. How could she ever?

She looked at Elysinia. "I understand. I know I must return to my world. I do not understand why right now, but I know you speak the truth. I have a purpose there. A purpose and a destiny that cannot be fulfilled here."

"Not only can it not be fulfilled here, but it is the reason that we, in this time, have hope." Elysinia smiled.

Jedda wondered. "Could you give him something for me? Something to remember me by?"

Elysinia just smiled in reply.

"Would you give him a rose for me?"
Elysinia smiled. "Yes, in a sense, I will."

Chapter 40
We Shall Meet Again

*"I am lying now in a meadow, holding the sky
in my arms. If I turn my gaze away from you,
Dear Earth, please do not feel hurt.
I will come back and kiss you again."*

—Rumi

The Forest – 11,000 BCE

Taivyn stood awaiting the one with whom he had most certainly fallen in love. He watched her enter into the circle of oak trees; then he saw her no more. An otherworldly mist rose up from the ground, not unlike the mist that had surrounded him in the meadow of flowers before he met the rose. The rose. Why did he think of her now?

Taivyn continued waiting patiently for his newly beloved. Alas, she did not return. He did not see her again. Not now. He wouldn't see her again for quite some time. Somehow, he knew that when she had entered the circle of trees, she wasn't coming back to him. He thought again about the rose, then back to Jedda.

Then someone did step from beyond the mists that shrouded the center of the circle of trees. It was not Jedda, but perhaps it was. It resembled her, but then it didn't. Her face was similar, and yet it wasn't. One noticeable difference was that her skin was sparkling white; it gave the appearance that it was filled with the dust of a thousand diamond chips. This one before him was surreal.

She took a few steps toward him, and his heart began to race. This girl or being (he wasn't sure which) extended her arm to him. In her hand, she held out a rose and said, "Until we meet again, My Beloved. Remember."

And then she was gone. She had somehow disappeared right before his eyes. He didn't understand what had occurred. He was filled with a love that he was unable to contain or control; it flowed in all directions and out to infinity. Taivyn turned to go. He knew he would eventually return to the Moon Clan community, but not just yet. He still didn't have the answers he sought. In fact, his journey thus far had only provoked more questions. Taivyn Green's whole life had changed in a matter of days. He wasn't the same boy who had left the community just days ago. When he did return, he would return as a courageous young man. Of this, nothing could be more certain.

Chapter 41
The Great Gathering

"It was magic…the whole sea was green fire
and white foam with singing mermaids in it.
And the Horses of the Hills picked their way
from one wave to another by lightning flashes!
That was the way it was in the old days!"

—Rudyard Kipling (1865–1936),
Rewards and Fairies

The Great Gathering Place – 11,000 BCE

T he moon was full and high in the sky; she smiled to the Earth as she sat watching over her. The light of her moonbeams was a silver blanket that both comforted and nurtured. The party of three finally arrived at their destination. The Great Gathering was a symbol of man and nature's ability to co-create. It was about collaboration, oneness, and partnership. It was about peace and hope. And most of all, it was about love.

Two immense standing stones marked the entranceway to the Great Gathering. These stones were ancient and had been placed here using the power of thought alone. The two stones were very unique and very different from one another. The first one on the left was male, and it was called Aradwar. On the right was Doramyn, and this stone was his female counterpart. The three stood looking in awe of these great Stone People.

Jory liked the rocks. He liked talking with them. They weren't complicated like humans. Of course, they were not complicated like gnomes either, for the stones did not even have to eat. He tried to fathom the idea of never being hungry. Yeah, that was definitely too much for him, especially with a growling stomach.

Lunaya placed her hand and her attention on Aradwar. She heard the familiar tone that signaled the connection of one spirit to the other. Everyone who came to the Great Gathering honored and connected with these stones before passing through. It was a tradition, and the stones held the memory of all the Great Gatherings that had ever been.

"Welcome, Lady Lunaya, daughter of the Moon, Keeper and elder of the Moon Clan."

"Thank you, Aradwar, for your warm welcome. We are here today to attend the Great Gathering. For our hearts have told us that the time has come. We wish to enter into this sacred time and sacred space."

"Enter, Lady Lunaya!"

Lunaya repeated this same process with the large stone on the right. Lunaya greeted Doramyn and connected with her spirit in the same way she had with Aradwar. The words were spoken again.

Each one in the party repeated this process. As they entered the place of the Great Gathering, they could see that all the others had already arrived and had taken their places. All but Elysinia. A wave of disappointment rushed over Master Ra-Ma'at. How was it that she was not present? She was, after all, the fifth council member of the Council of Five.

The Council of Five was a council of Faery elders, one for each of the four elements that manifest in form; the fifth element was Spirit or Love. They nodded to each of the new arrivals as a sign of warm welcome. Master Ra-Ma'at was thrilled to see them, as it had been ages since they'd all last met. He looked around to see who else had shown up. There were other Faery beings there. Some of them he easily recognized, while others were new faces. The treetops were filled with twinkling faery lights belonging to the hundreds of nature spirits of the Forest. Several gnomes tipped their pointed hats in greeting. Even the Aluxes, the mysterious beings from the land across the Great Sea, were present. Highly unusual was the multitude of animals that had joined this occasion—there were rabbits, a platypus, a family of wolves, and other small and interesting creatures popping in here and there. Strange that some of the elders from the Moon Clan were not in attendance. Only Telzar, Lir, and Astriel could be seen amongst the crowd. They waved in recognition. Then Ra-Ma'at saw the bear from earlier that day.

"Glad you could finally make it. You know bears don't fancy waiting too long for anything?" the bear growled in jest. He was actually in high spirits. "I see you were able to connect with your sister." The bear glanced over at the Lady Lunaya and greeted her warmly before turning back to Ra-Ma'at. "Any luck finding the boy?"

"Not yet. I will speak about it to Elysinia after the meeting. Where is she anyway?"

"Not sure. I believe they mean to address that shortly."

A lizard took a seat in front on a tall branch of an ash tree just in time. Leori, the first Council member spoke: "Greetings to you all. We thank you all for coming. We rejoice in this reunion of old and new faces alike. There are some who have been added to our Great Gathering, and some who have gone on to the land of the Eternal Sun. They have crossed over and thus we will take a moment to honor those who have gone before us and those who have carried this tradition of co-creative partnership between Faery and Humans throughout the ages. We thank you!"

With that all the attendees closed their eyes. They used this time to move into the sacred space of their hearts. From their hearts, they connected to the Earth and to the Heavens. In loving gratitude, they honored those who had gone before them, as well as all Life everywhere.

"I know we are anxious to move to the first order of business, but before we do, I know you all have been wondering about the whereabouts of Elysinia, one of the elders of the Faery People, She Who Holds Within Her The Fifth Element, our Record Keeper. It was imperative that she attend to something of great importance before joining us here today. In fact, it is concerning the reason we are all here. So I would ask that you all be patient, because she will be arriving shortly, and we do not wish to begin without her, nor would it be correct to do so."

Leori concluded his speech for the time being. He was the elder of the Fire Clan. He was fierce, bold, and he was on fire literally. His body reflected the light of the stars as did the other Faery Ones; however, small bursts of tiny flames would ignite periodically. His hair was a brilliant coppery orange. From a distance, one might confuse it for a lion's mane or even a small conflagration. His fingers surged with sparks, and when he spoke, the little flares danced around him.

Fire was the element Leori governed, or was governed by, depending on how one looked at it. It was he who had taught the humans about this great gift many moons ago. He carried a staff-like wand in his hand that was representative of this element. One of the original Faery Hallows, this staff held within it the power of transmutation and purification. Master Ra-Ma'at had spent a great deal of time studying with him in order to master the fire element. For where else might a great Solar Keeper learn about fire but from the elder Faery of the Fire Clan himself?

The buzz was felt, and everyone waited with anticipation, for they knew that Elysinia was not late by accident. They all knew that whatever she was involved in had everything to do with this meeting and possibly would determine this gathering's outcome.

Chapter 42
The Fifth Sacred Thing

"Through humanity's free will choice, life could consciously join with the living Earth Mother who was already beginning to align her consciousness to her ascending return into the higher realms of light and union."

—Claire Heartsong,
Anna, Grandmother of Jesus

The Gathering Place – 11,000 BCE

Then a sonic sound was felt and heard throughout the land. The sound could be nothing else than the signal of Elysinia's arrival. She had just approached the standing stones, and, as was customary, she participated in the same tradition that each of the others had done before passing through into the Great Gathering place, for she was no exception. The tone was that of liquid rainbow and chimes of golden light—it was an audible hum that toned the chant of life.

Then, suddenly, a second tone was heard and felt throughout the land. There was a magnificent white light that poured into the Great Gathering area and with it the eternal sound of all creation. The light could be felt by each one.

The time had come for the Great Gathering to truly commence. Elysinia appeared in the center of the space, a vision of mystical enchantment. The white light illuminated her form, and she appeared to give off a radiant glow. She was beautiful. All honored her arrival by bowing. It was a demonstration of their love and great respect for this Ancient One. She was the Record Keeper, for it was she who accessed and read the rings within the trees. And it was she who then activated crystals that would store that information for generations to come. It was a beautiful gift and honor to do this work, and no other did it like Elysinia.

Tears of joy and sadness fell from Ra-Ma'at's eyes all at once. He had been harboring feelings of regret for half a century. He lovingly gazed at her, as though they were the only two in this place. In that moment, she read his thoughts and heart, and she smiled in acknowledgment and knowing. They had always been one. She had to leave because she had a great work to do, especially seeing that the portal was coming to a close.

Elysinia had known the time had come when the veil would separate the worlds. Much of the magic would go to sleep on one side of the veil. Many would forget. Many of the beings of light would have to leave the third dimension of the Earth plane. Of course, many knew this, but she saw it from a slightly elevated perspective. It was her responsibility to see to it that this did not become a missed opportunity, and that some remnant of hope and magic still existed in the mundane world beyond the Forest and beyond the Faery Mists.

So overwhelmed was he with emotion that Ra-Ma'at wept uncontrollably. He had not expected to have a physical display of emotions such as this. He had missed her so much. All those years of regret and despair can have that effect sometimes. Elysinia directed a ray of love and Faery Light to his heart; he received and reciprocated with gladness. They smiled at one another once again. Ra-Ma'at's tears began to subside, and he felt peace. Then she spoke. When she did, she addressed all who were present.

"I want to thank you all for hearing the call within your own hearts and souls to attend this meeting. As you know, the Age of Light is gradually coming to a close; the Age of Darkness that brings sleep to the hearts and minds of men, and even sleep to the Earth, is fast approaching. The Earth herself is preparing for a time of hibernation, and when she awakens at the other end of the cycle approximately 13,000 years later, she will be ready to take her ascension. This time span seems great, but I assure you, that it is only a blink of an eye in the great cycles of the ages upon the Earth and within the galaxy.

"Unlike other cycles gone before, this one comes with a unique set of challenges and obstacles. The time we foresee within the rings of the trees—and I have imprinted the crystal with these images for all of you to observe—is one of great darkness and forgetting."

She paused there to present the crystal as it materialized in the center of the Gathering place. This crystal was mostly clear, with smoky hues of charcoal grey that swirled within it. It was immense, as it stood the height of an elephant. As each of the attendees gazed into its depths, images of light were reflected into their mind's eye. They only saw those images that were meant for them. It was unfiltered information, and yet one could only see what their level of consciousness would allow. After everyone had viewed the upcoming cycle in a way that was befitting for each one, Elysinia continued.

"There is an event occurring with many of the brothers and sisters in the Atlantian continent right now that is going to change life as we know it. It will even affect the great Earth Mother's grid. It is not ours to intervene or change, but, alas, we shall all be affected by it."

Elysinia knew that the information she shared was very new to some, and so she allowed time for it to sink in and take root. She looked to her brothers and sisters of the Faery Race. She looked to Vayu, the elder of the Air Clan who floated beside her with grace.

Vayu was barely visible; so much a part of the wind was he. His ephemeral white robes were filled with light and wind and blew gently in some breeze only felt by him. To the side of his waist, he carried a sheath, which bore a hilt at the top. All knew that this sheath carried within it the Sword of Truth, the Faery Hallow of the Air Clan. Vayu smiled at Elysinia, showing his support for her and everything that she was saying. Elysinia continued.

"I do not share this news about the Atlantian brothers and sisters to bring distress or fear. Rather, I share this in light of a newfound hope. Many of you may have felt or heard the song that signals the Crossing of the Frog and the Mushroom. I am here to tell you that it is true, and I have witnessed it with my own eyes. The time of their crossing is near. The frog and the mushroom are indeed in preparation to cross paths. Of course, many of you understand the magnitude of this event. It is an event of power. However, we must keep this meeting of two souls out of the hands of those who would use the energy and power for self. As you know, the moment of their crossing can be used to transform the movements of the Mushroom into power. This power is unbridled and raw. It would destroy most.

"However, you also know that this event brings with it a great opportunity for transformation and evolution, for the power wielded from it can also be a great catalyst for good. If utilized correctly, it could be a very effective tool for awakening. And so, I bring you my proposition for Healing.

"Rose, could you come forward please."

Rose stepped out from behind the folds. Her hair was like rainbow strands of silk that graced the floor as she walked. Upon her form, she wore an emerald gown; it streamed in layers of color and light that twirled around her as she moved. Rose looked lovingly at her mother. She nodded her understanding, for she knew the destiny that lay before her. It was a great undertaking. Rose knew within that while the journey that she had been on was coming to an end, another was just beginning.

"For those of you who do not know her, I present my daughter Rose. Rose has agreed to what I am about to propose, for this idea has not yet been done in the history of the Earth, as far as the records have shown me. It is a great work with a great purpose that Rose has agreed to carry out. Afterward, if there are others who wish to join her on this journey, you may stand forth then and when the time is right."

Elysinia looked at her daughter with tears in her eyes, for she knew that what lay ahead was to be arduous—a path filled with many thorns and briar patches. She did not know what the journey would hold for her exactly, but she knew that it would be sad and lonely, and eventually even Rose would forget. One thing was now certain, Rose would awaken one day and remember.

Rose looked at her mother with tender reassurance that she fully understood, at least as much as she could, the impact and possible consequences of this choice. Elysinia nodded and continued.

"What Rose has agreed to is this: We will channel the energy and power of the mushroom's movements that the Crossing gifts us with in such a way as to create a bridge of rainbow light from our world—the world of the Forest and the world of Faerie—to the human world. Rose will walk that bridge of rainbow light, and at the end, will step off taking her first step into the human evolutionary path of consciousness."

The whole gathering gasped. There were hushed whispers and chatter among them. No one had seen this coming. For what Elysinia was essentially saying was that Rose would give up her immortality and give up her Faery Light in an effort to become human. They could not believe it. They could not even understand it completely.

Then it was Seamone's turn to speak. Born of the ocean, Seamone was the elder of the Water Clan. She glided forward so she could be heard. As she did, waves of cerulean light glittered around her. Her gown was one of watery rivulets of ocean blues and turquoise greens. It carried with it the sound of the sea as she walked. Golden locks that looked like waterfalls swirled about and crowned her face. Her hair was adorned with seashells and sapphires that shimmered in the light of the stars. She floated on a cushion of sea foam that glided around her and rose up in tiny bubbles. Around her neck hung a golden chalice, the Faery Hallow of the Water Clan. She stepped forward to speak and be heard.

"Elysinia, while I do honor your plan and the choice that Rose has made, I must ask: what purpose does it serve other than imprinting the idea of a new experience into race consciousness? How does this serve to help us with the impending Dark part of the Cycle and the darkness that is upon us and the Earth?"

Elysinia responded confidently but lovingly and with a great respect. "Thank you, Seamone, for voicing this question, as I am sure it is upon the minds of many here today. Of course, it will enrich Rose's soul experience on an individual level, for isn't that the purpose of a soul's journey—to create different experiences in life?

"However, the purpose for Rose's crossover, as it will be called, is much greater than sheer gain of a new experience. The reason for her crossover is beneficial on a planetary scale. For even though she will be human, she will have and hold within her a Faery Heart. This heart she will carry through many incarnations, and eventually the Age of Sleep will touch even her and she will forget. However, at the right and perfect time, when the Wheel of the Ages turns and the Age of Light comes around again, this Faery Heart will activate and awaken. And then, my Dear Ones, Rose will remember. In this way, the teachings will be preserved, and not just the teachings but the memory of living in harmony and oneness with nature. Rose will awaken, and she will teach others to do the same. She will carry this memory deep within her Faery Heart, and, at the appropriate time, it will begin to shine Faery Light once again."

There was a buzzing energy that ran through the hearts of those present. The energy ranged from excitement to sadness. It was an incredible feat, and yet it was brilliant.

Ra-Ma'at allowed tears to flow again. He understood now why Elysinia had left all those years ago—to spend each and every moment that she had left with her daughter, for it might be a great long time before she would see her again. Rose was not his daughter. She was birthed long before they had come together, and, in the Faery Race, birth need only take place with the female intention.

Ra-Ma'at felt such closure and relief, because in that moment, he knew that Elysinia had not walked out on them or their love. She left to return to her one and only daughter—to prepare her for the task that laid ahead. She must have known that one day she would have to give up her sweet Rosebud.

It was no longer important whether or not he and Elysinia came back together again in this life or the next. He knew she loved him, and her wisdom was beyond what he could have ever comprehended.

And so, at that Great Gathering, it was decided that Rose would cross over from Faerie into Human consciousness to experience yet another level of expression on Gaia, the planet Earth.

Then it was Aolana, the elder of the Earth Clan, who stepped forward. Not unlike the other Shining Ones, Aolana's skin was sparkling in the light of the moon. However, because of her exquisite mastery of all things terrestrial, it had taken on a virescent sheen. Her emerald eyes mesmerized any who dared to hold her gaze. Vines, the color of jade, wrapped and twisted around her arms. Extraordinarily long hair, in earth shades of rust and terra cotta, tumbled down her back and over her shoulders. As if playing a game of hide-and-seek, tiny flowers peaked out from beneath the dramatic tendrils. Like a moving garden of delicate blossoms and verdant leaves, her gown rustled in harmony with the gentle Night Forest's song.

Aolana had within her outstretched hand a circular disk-like stone. She held it up to Rose and said, "Receive the blessing of the Great Earth Mother. For your choice and your work is honored. Know that you will always be supported even if you don't know it or remember. You are greatly loved, Dear One, daughter of the Earth and all her elements. Take the energy of this Faery Hallow into your heart as a memory. We love you."

Now, it was Rose's turn to cry. She felt so much love and support from her Faery Kin. And she could see the love and admiration the human and animal attendees had for her and her upcoming journey as well. She thanked Aolana, for the blessing of the Stone of Destiny. Then Leori, Vayu, and Seamone approached Rose. They each offered her the blessing of their respective element.

Filled with gratitude, Rose turned to her mother. "Mother, I love you." She looked around, "I love all of you, and it is for you that I will do this, for us, for all of us. It is an honor and my great pleasure to serve."

Elysinia's eyes mirrored something close to joy and heartache. She turned to the others. "Are there any of you who wish to join my Rosebud on her journey? You will know in your hearts if the call is yours to answer."

With that invitation, there were several brave souls who stood forth, but those Faery souls' journeys are another story. For this was the story of the Rose.

Chapter 43
Remember—The End of the Beginning

*"At the edge of our dreams the faeries stand
and wait in reflective vigil. They have waited so
long, and yet so few of us have willingly crossed
over the threshold."*

—Brian Froud, *World of Faerie*

Maine – 2004

Jedda awoke lying in her bed. She wasn't sure how she had gotten back, but she had. She felt refreshed, revitalized, and charged with a sense of purpose. It was like she had just reclaimed a missing part of herself. There was a pervading sense of wonder and levity that made her believe that she could bounce atop clouds and not fall through them. She checked behind her to see if she had grown wings (or if they had returned), because she was ready for takeoff. To what and to where, she did not know, but she was ready to start the day.

She suddenly wondered if it had all been a dream; it didn't really matter, though. For what it was worth, it was real, even if only in her heart. She got up ready to start the day and launch into whatever lay ahead. Nothing really mattered, and yet everything did. She looked outside her window and saw Artemis sitting over by the willow tree. She dashed out of her room and rushed down the stairs. Her mother raised an eyebrow. She would never completely understand her daughter. She shook her head and smiled.

Jedda grabbed the knob to the front door and twisted it. She flung the door open wide, as if it were light as a feather, for that was how Jedda felt. She ran across the front lawn and over to the edge of the driveway where the willow tree grew tall.

Artemis looked up and meowed, "Jedda, you are home! I have been waiting for you. I knew you would come back to me, my Keeper! I thought you would arrive through the tree, but I guess I must've missed your return somehow. Although I'm not sure how, because I haven't moved an inch since you left and…"

Jedda was ecstatic. She couldn't believe her ears. "Artemis, you can talk? I can't believe it. That means it wasn't all a dream, was it? It was all very real. Why have I not heard you until now?"

Artemis smiled a wry smile and said very matter-of-factly, "Oh, because I don't talk very much."

Jedda started crying again. It seemed that was all she did lately, but this time they were tears of elation. Jedda glanced up. She saw the raven roosting on one of the hanging branches. He was staring at her, and he had a glimmer in his eye.

"You remember now," he said.

Jedda smiled. Her blue eyes sparkled in the light of the sun. Her heart felt so full with the essence of gratitude that suffused her, for what had once been lost had now been retrieved. She responded, "Yes. Now I remember."

Then he continued, "Good! Because, Jedda, let it be known that this is only the beginning!" He let out a big caw and took flight, soaring until he disappeared out of sight.

The Beginning

Made in the USA
Middletown, DE
13 September 2020

19496054R00170